"I have come to reclaim my wife."

Lexi's breath caught in her throat at his sheer arrogance. No way would she put herself back in the subservient position of being Jake's wife. "I won't tolerate it."

Jake slowly strolled across the room. "No more than I will tolerate some curt note from a lawyer telling me I am to be divorced. You, Lexi, are my wife, and divorce is not an option. Not now, not ever. Do I make myself clear?"

JACQUELINE BAIRD began writing as a hobby when her family objected to the smell of her oil painting, and immediately became hooked on the romantic genre. She loves traveling, and worked her way around the world from Europe to the Americas and Australia, returning to England to marry her sweetheart. She lives in the north-east of England, where she was born, and has two grown-up sons. She enjoys sports, and spends most weekends with husband Jim, sailing on their small boat.

Books by Jacqueline Baird

HARLEQUIN PRESENTS
1359—SHATTERED TRUST
1431—PASSIONATE BETRAYAL
1558—DISHONOURABLE PROPOSAL
1683—MASTER OF PASSION
1726—GAMBLE ON PASSION

JACQUELINE BAIRD

Nothing Changes Love

Harlequin Books

TORONTO • NEW YORK • LONDON
AMSTERDAM • PARIS • SYDNEY • HAMBURG
STOCKHOLM • ATHENS • TOKYO • MILAN
MADRID • WARSAW • BUDAPEST • AUCKLAND

ISBN 0-373-11757-4

NOTHING CHANGES LOVE

First North American Publication 1995.

This edition published by arrangement with Harlequin Enterprises B.V.

® and TM are trademarks of the publisher. Trademarks indicated with
® are registered in the United States Patent and Trademark Office, the
Canadian Trade Marks Office and in other countries.

Printed in U.S.A.

CHAPTER ONE

LEXI opened her eyes and for a moment was completely disorientated. White walls, a narrow bed, white sheets, and the smell...antiseptic!

She moved to sit up, and the full horror of the past night sliced into her heart. She groaned with the unaccustomed pain and dragged herself up to a sitting position, her small hands clutching the white weave of the coverlet.

Her baby, the tiny being growing inside her only twenty-four hours ago, was no more. She had miscarried; after all the expert care and bed rest, nothing had been able to save her precious child. Moisture flooded her violet eyes, and with the back of her hand she brushed it away.

'Now, now, Lexi, try not to upset yourself too much.'

She looked up at the familiar figure of a Dr Bell, a tall, balding man; he had been her doctor for all her twenty years, but even he had been helpless to prevent her losing her first baby, a boy... She tried to smile but it was a watery effort.

'Some things in life, child, are just not meant to be.' He took one of her small hands in his, his world-weary eyes scanning the small, beautiful figure in the bed. He could remember the day she was born, tiny and squalling, with a shock of brilliant red hair. She had developed into a bright, incredibly beautiful young woman and she did not deserve the grief she had borne for the past few years. He had hoped that with her marriage not a year ago her luck had finally turned, but in that it seemed he was mistaken; her high-flying husband had not even bothered to attend the hospital last night, although he had been informed of the imminent loss of the baby.

'But I so wanted my baby,' Lexi moaned.

'It is tragic to lose a baby at fourteen weeks, but there is always a reason, nature's way of letting us know something is not quite right. But you're young and perfectly fit; there will be many more babies for you. The important thing is not to worry about it.'

'If you say so.' But the flat, toneless quality of her voice told the doctor the poor girl was not convinced.

'Anyway, that handsome husband of yours will be here shortly. I have spoken to him personally.'

'Jake knows?' she queried quietly.

'Yes, and the two of you together will soon see this as a sad memory, nothing more, once you fill Forest Manor with a few healthy children.' He smiled and, straightening up, he let go of her hand. 'Believe me; after all, I am the expert.'

A commotion, raised voices in the corridor outside the small private room, prevented Lexi making any reply. The door swung open and a tall, dark man rushed into the room. Pushing Dr Bell aside, he sat down on the side of the bed, and gathered Lexi's small hands in his much larger ones.

'God! Lexi, I'm so sorry, I know how much the baby meant to you; I can't believe it has happened.'

'Jake.' She murmured his name. 'It wasn't my fault.' She wanted to explain, but couldn't find the words. Her violet eyes roamed over his handsome face, the night-black hair curling haphazardly over his broad brow, as though he had never had time to brush it. His dark eyes that at first glance looked brown but on closer inspection were almost navy blue, were fixed on her small face, the concern in his expression undeniable. Jake, her husband; he looked so dynamic, so vitally alive, and she felt dead inside. An aching void where her child should have been.

'Shh, darling, don't try and talk. I'm here now, I will look after you.'

But would he? The question popped into her mind, she did not know from where. Lexi had needed him last night, had cried out for him in her agony, but where had he been? Giving a dinner party for clients...

'Did your meeting with the Americans, the Stewarts wasn't it, go well?' she asked quietly.

Jake sat up straighter, his clasp of her hands loosening. 'More or less.'

'Which was it?' Lexi queried, somehow aware the worried frown marring his brow wasn't solely for her.

His hand tightened on hers but his smile was forced as he answered. 'One or two problems, but nothing I can't handle. Don't concern yourself, Lexi. Let me worry about the business. The important thing is for you to get better and out of this tiny cottage hospital as quickly as possible.'

'What kind of problem?' she asked mechanically.

Jake turned his dark head to Dr Bell and deliberately changed the subject with, 'I wanted Lexi to go to Harley Street, but she insisted on you, and I want some answers, and I want them now. Why wasn't I informed last night when this happened?' And, getting to his feet, Lexi ignored for the moment, the two men stood face to face.

'According to our records, the sister on duty telephoned the manor at nine last night. You were unavailable at the time, but my sister was assured you would be given the message.'

'I don't believe it; I demand to see the administrator, and I'll make damn sure heads roll for this.'

Lexi closed her eyes briefly, trying to block out the image of a furious Jake, but it was impossible. She looked at him, all six feet plus of bristling male aggression. He was wearing a short-sleeved knit shirt in pale blue that fit snugly across his wide shoulders and broad chest. A black leather belt slung low on his hips supported well-washed denim jeans that clung lovingly to his long, muscular legs. The father of her baby, and yet, when he had arrived, he had said he knew how much the baby meant to her. How she wished he had said, 'us', and swept her into his arms; she ached to lay her head on his broad chest and forget yesterday had ever happened.

She tuned back into the conversation in time to hear Dr Bell demand, 'Do you really think this is the time or the place for this discussion, Mr Taylor?'

Lexi's bemused gaze went from one man to the other, not sure who to believe; she wanted to believe Jake.

'You're right, Dr Bell,' Jake agreed curtly. 'But don't think you have heard the last of this.'

'Please, Jake,' she reached out a trembling hand 'No recriminations, I couldn't bear it.'

'Oh, hell! I'm sorry, Lexi,' and swooping down, at last he cradled her in his strong arms. 'Forgive me darling, it's just I'm so angry, I wasn't here when you needed me. No business deal is worth a fraction of what you mean to me.' He tilted her head back to look into her bruised eyes. 'You do know that, darling?' With one long, tanned finger he traced the soft curve of her cheek, the dark circles under her eyes, then softly his sensuous mouth brushed lightly against hers.

'Yes, Jake, of course,' she murmured huskily, her voice thick with tears. But did she? the errant thought flashed in her mind. She glanced up at him and was stunned to see moisture glistening on his thick black lashes.

'I called last night, after midnight, and they told me you were asleep. If only I'd known.' His deep voice shook with emotion.

'It's all right.' But he could have asked about the baby; if he weren't such a workaholic he might have done. She banished the disloyal thought and added, 'You're here now and that's all that matters.'

For a long moment their eyes clung. Pain, regret and deep sorrow; the message passed between them, too agonising to put into words.

'There will be other children, love.' Jake cradled her head against his broad shoulder, his strong hand smoothing the wild tangle of red curls back from her face and gently down her back in the age-old gesture of comfort. 'Cry if you need to, Lexi, let it all out.' His deep, rich voice murmured soft words of comfort and consolation.

To Lexi it was the care she needed and, held close in Jake's arms, the familiar scent and feel of him enveloping her, she cried as though her heart would break. Finally, all cried out, she hiccuped and raised swollen red eyes to his handsome face.

'I'll be all right now.'

'We both will be; together we can beat whatever the world throws at us.' His dark head lowered and his mouth claimed hers in an achingly gentle kiss.

Lexi curled her slender arms around his neck, needing him as never before. His sensuous lips, warm and mobile, moved seductively over hers, his tongue slipping erotically into her mouth. Surprised by his turning the kiss from gentle to passionate, she tensed, inexplicably revolted. Jake groaned against her mouth, a flare of desire sharp and instant tautened his huge frame, and, pulling back, he looked down into her pale face.

'God! What am I doing? You're ill, you need rest.' He pressed her back down against the pillows, and shifted his tall body uncomfortably on the bed. 'It never fails. From the first day I saw you, I only have to look at you to want you.' A rueful self-deprecating smile twisted his firm lips. 'I shall have to learn to control my baser instincts around you, at least for a while,' he teased lightly.

Lexi attempted a smile, but unsettling questions niggled at the edge of her mind. Was that all Jake wanted from her? A warm body in his bed? Was that all he had ever wanted? Their baby, a mistake!

Half an hour later, after Jake had left, promising to return in the evening, Lexi was informed by Dr Bell that she could leave the next day. She should have been pleased, instead all she felt was a mind-numbing exhaustion and physical weakness that made the thought of leaving the security of the hospital for their apartment and the bustle of the hotel, and the inevitable condolences of the staff, a terrifying prospect.

A deep, drawn-out sigh escaped her. It was so unfair, she thought hopelessly. On Friday afternoon she had been a happy, pregnant mum-to-be. She had driven into York to keep an appointment at four with Dr Bell, just routine, but first she had gone shopping for something glamorous to wear at the dinner party she was hosting the following night with her husband at Forest Manor. The manor, once her childhood home, had been converted by Jake's property company into a country house hotel. Now only the west wing was home.

Unfortunately, it had started to rain, and, dashing to keep her doctor's appointment, she had slipped on the wet pavement and fallen. She had jumped to her feet and run on, arriving at the surgery late and rather upset. Dr Bell had examined her, and said she was spotting a little, and insisted she stay in the local hospital for a day or two just as a precaution.

Lexi, slightly in awe of her sophisticated, dynamic husband, had dreaded telling him. She knew Jake was hoping to make a deal with Mr Stewart, an American tycoon who owned, among other things, his own airline, along with a tour firm that ran regular trips to England. Jake had explained that if Mr Stewart agreed to use the new Forest Manor hotel as a regular stop for his clients, the hotel was assured of being at least half-full all year, even if it never got another customer. A great deal if Jake could get it.

She need not have worried, because Jake had arrived on the Friday night from London and been a tower of strength, telling her not to worry, his PA, Lorraine, could host the party and all Lexi had to do was look after herself and the baby.

Lexi turned restlessly on the narrow bed. How could life change so drastically from Friday to Sunday? All her hopes and dreams squashed by a wet pavement. It seemed so pointless...

'Come on, Mrs Taylor. Cheer up.' The sister who had attended her the night before walked in. 'You're young, and time heals all wounds. I know you don't think so at the minute, but it is true. And it's also true that I did ring your home last night; a woman answered and promised to give your husband the message.'

Lexi looked at the sister, and she knew Jake's hand was in the unsolicited statement somewhere.

'The young woman sounded supremely efficient; I never doubted for a moment she would pass the message on.'

It could only have been Lorraine, Lexi thought resignedly. 'It's all right, Sister, I believe you. My husband has been in this morning. Everything is fine.'

'I wish you would tell him that.'

Lexi heard the sister mutter under her breath as she left the room, and felt sorry for her. Lexi knew personally just how intimidating Jake could be if he thought he had been wronged in any way. She still shuddered to think of the way he had dismissed the foreman on the hotel project last Christmas, frog-marching the man to his car and tossing his gear in with him. Jake was not the sort of man one argued with. Lexi had never tried; far too much in love with him, she would do anything to appease him.

Now, why did that thought make her feel even more depressed? she mused. Maybe losing the baby had made her realise once again how fragile life was, and question her slavish acceptance to everything Jake said or did. She tossed her head to dispel the unsettling notion, and the bedroom door swung open to reveal what looked like a walking basket of flowers.

The junior nurse dropped it on the floor with a sigh of relief and a huge smile. 'Somebody out there loves you,' she teased.

Lexi eyed the huge basket with wonder. Masses of roses tastefully arranged with babies' breath and the message on the card was simple. 'Love always, Jake.' The briefest of smiles curved her lips. Just like him: larger than life.

Alone once more, Lexi turned over on to her side, her violet eyes fixed firmly on the flowers. The aching sense of loss was still there, but somehow it did not seem quite so devastating, as long as she had Jake. She smiled softly remembering the first time they met, perhaps it was the mind's way of dealing with a hurt too hard to face, she mused, as she drifted in a dream-state, recalling the past in minute detail. At nineteen years of age, and having just completed her first-year exams in languages at St Mary's college, London, Lexi had been called back to her home, Forest Manor, because of her father's sudden death. Her mother had died three years earlier, only weeks after her father had retired from the Diplomatic Corps. Laughtons had for generations entered the foreign service, and between postings lived in Yorkshire.

The house was a beautiful old stone-built manor. E-shaped, with mullioned windows, oak floors and beautiful hand-carved panelling and situated seven miles from the cathedral city of York, mid-way between the tiny villages of Sand Hutton and Stockton-on-the-Forest.

But on the death of her father his substantial pension had ceased, and the lawyer had informed Lexi that his personal debts were quite large. As one of the Lloyds names her father had enjoyed a good private income for years, but a few years previously he had changed syndicates hoping to make even bigger profits.

Unfortunately the reverse had happened, and Lexi had had no alternative but to put the house and its extensive parkland on the market to cover the debt.

Lexi turned over on to her back and stared sightlessly up at the blank white ceiling. It seemed incredible to believe it was under a year since she had first met Jake. She felt as if she had known him a lifetime, so much had happened.

It was a beautiful July day. Lexi waited in the entrance porch of her home, and watched as a sleek black car drew to a halt in front of the door and the tall figure of a man stepped out.

'Mr Taylor?' she queried as the man bounded up the stone steps to stop only inches away from her.

'Yes, and you must be Alexandra Laughton. Your solicitor said you were young, but he didn't mention beautiful.'

'Lexi, please. No one calls me Alexandra,' she said nervously and blushed scarlet, embarrassed by his frank compliment, and also by the overpowering effect the man had on her. He looked about thirty, and was dressed in a plain white shirt, dark tie and an immaculate three-piece business suit, the jacket stretched taut across broad shoulders and a massive chest. His hair was black and thick, and his face alert and hard. There was no mistaking the fierce predatory expression on his roughly hewn features. A broad forehead, deep dark eyes, high cheek bones and a straight blade of a nose above a wide, firm mouth. His skin was the colour of polished mahogany.

'I'm afraid I'm in rather a hurry. So, shall we proceed?' he said briskly, all business.

'Y-yes. Yes, of course,' she stammered, leading him into the panelled entrance hall. 'You're very brown. Are you English?' God! Where had that come from? She cringed; it was totally out of character for Lexi to pass personal comments and she turned red with embarrassment. 'Please...'

To her surprise he started to laugh and, catching one of her small hands in his, he said, 'Jake Taylor, luv... Born within the sound of the Bow Bells. A cockney, a tanned cockney, though I believe my father was a foreigner.' He drawled the last word teasingly.

He was laughing at her but she could not blame him; so far she had not managed to make much sense. Lexi shook her head in a vain attempt to clear her brain, and her long red hair spun around her face in a glittering cloud before settling back on her slender shoulders. She had dressed with care, expecting the first prospective buyer for the house, in a plain, shirt-style straight-skirted cream summer-dress. She had added a minimum of make-up to her golden skin; she was one of those very rare redheads with a skin that actually tanned. Her full lips were carefully outlined in a soft coral lip gloss and a touch of mascara on her long lashes completed her make-up and she'd thought she appeared quite adult, until this man had looked at her.

'I'm sorry, that was presumptuous of me. Please, follow me, and I'll show you around.' Her violet eyes met his once more, and she felt the intensity of his gaze to the soles of her feet. She again shook her head, but nothing could clear her mind and she spent the next hour leading him around the half-dozen reception rooms, up the grand staircase, all around the upper floors until finally they arrived back in the hall with Lexi still in a bemused state.

'Are you free for the rest of the day?'

'What? Oh, yes.' Lexi had to get her brain in gear, but it seemed to be an impossibility. 'But why?' she asked, standing once more in the front porch. Common sense told her he should leave: he was too dynamic, too male, and certainly too sophisticated for her. She felt oddly threatened by him, but her foolishly fast-beating heart wanted him to stay.

'Good. I had only allowed an hour for our meeting; now I think I'll make a day of it and you can show me around the countryside, then I can get the feel of the place. You understand.'

She didn't understand at all, but her heart leapt in her breast at the prospect of spending the whole day with the man. Before she could agree or disagree Jake had ushered her into his car and slid in beside her. He made a call on the car-phone to someone called Lorraine, who seemed less than pleased at his extended visit, Lexi thought, then he turned to her.

'Now, I am your willing tourist until late this evening, or, if you prefer, tomorrow morning.' And, flicking her a blatantly sensual smile, he asked, 'Which way to Castle Howard? I've heard it's worth seeing.'

The faint spicy tang of his aftershave teased her nostrils, and for some reason his sexy grin appeared to heighten her awareness of him in a way no other man had ever managed to do before. She was not a complete innocent; she had a good social life at college and she had had her fair share of dates, but Jake Taylor was something else again, and she found the emotion he aroused in her enthralling.

Twenty minutes later they were driving up the impressive drive through the entrance gates and into the large field-like car park of Castle Howard.

'Good, it's near your place,' she heard Jake murmur as he helped her out of the car, his eyes darting all around, taking everything in.

Jake flung a casual arm around her shoulders. 'I think this might just be the clincher,' he opined and, paying the admission fee, urged Lexi through to the courtyard while she was still trying to fathom out what he meant.

For the next few hours she walked around in a dream. Jake strode around the elegant house, his hand never leaving her shoulder as he talked non-stop to her, pointing out the things that really grabbed his interest, from the magnificent domed roof in the grand hall, unique in all of England, to the quaint child's high chair. Castle Howard was magnificent: the furnishings, the restoration, works of art—everything about the place was exquisite. A superb example of eighteenth-century architecture, it was built by the Third Earl of Carlisle, and to the present day was still owned by the same family of Howards. Lexi had visited many times before, but today the awesome grandeur of the place was overwhelmed by her intense awareness of her companion.

To Lexi's surprise Jake seemed almost as impressed by the wide variety of tourists—Americans and Japanese rubbed shoulders with continentals—as he was with the house itself, and finally, when they walked back outside into the summer sunshine and strolled around the extensive grounds, Jake had no compunction in striking up conversations with dozens of people, while Lexi looked around at the wonderful landscape, long lawns, magnificent lakes, summer house, and, high on one hill, the family mausoleum. It wasn't hard to see, she thought, why it had achieved worldwide recognition as the location for the television serial *Brideshead Revisited*. Perched on the Howardian Hills, it had to be one of the best stately homes in England.

'Penny for your thoughts.'

She looked up and smiled into Jake's darkly handsome face. 'They aren't worth much, but I am hungry,' she stated. 'Walking gives me an appetite.'

'You give me an appetite,' Jake growled huskily and, before she realised his intention, he had turned her into his arms, and brushed his hard mouth gently across her full lips. It was like being touched by lightning; a shiver trembled the length of her spine and her full lips parted helplessly beneath his. The breath hissed out of him. 'God!' he exclaimed, as he broke the kiss.

He held her away from him, studying her flushed, bemused face. 'I've been aching to do that from the minute I set eyes on you. You have a very unsettling effect on me, little girl. But this is not the place.' Knowing full well how he affected her, he grinned reassuringly down into her wide violet eyes, and, curving her arm under his, led her back to the car.

She wasn't used to a handsome sophisticated man like Jake flirting with her and, during the journey to the city of York where Jake had insisted they visit next, she couldn't think of a word to say. But somehow the atmosphere between them was a companionable one, and by the time they arrived in York and found the car park Lexi had recovered some of her poise.

It seemed quite natural to walk hand in hand around the mighty cathedral, and then follow the narrow streets around the Shambles. Finally, they ended up in a small French restaurant with the original name of Number 19 Grape Lane, and, over a lovely meal of pan-fried salmon on a bed of pasta in a red wine sauce—Jake's choice— he enthusiastically explained his plan for Forest Manor. He wanted to buy it and turn it into a hotel, and shrewdly he asked her if she would take it off the market for a week or two while he had a feasibility study carried out.

He could have knocked it down for all Lexi cared; for the first time in her life she was in love. Hopelessly, helplessly in love. Her gaze lingered on his striking features as he set out his ideas for the conversion; he looked years younger as, with a sheepish grin, he ended with, 'Sorry, I can get quite boring when I start discussing business.'

'No, you're fascinating,' she said softly, and the deepening gleam in his dark eyes set her heart ablaze. Jake was everything she had ever dreamed of in a man, and best of all he appeared to feel the same way, if the goodnight kiss he pressed on her lips when they parted

at her door was anything to go by, and his promise to
return the next day.

The only slight hiccup in her headlong flight into love
was her solicitor. On Monday morning she called Mr
Travis and told him what had happened and that she
did not want anyone else viewing the house for a while.
Mr Travis was not convinced it was the right thing to
do, and insisted he had friends in the city and a few
discreet enquiries were called for. Taylor Holdings was
not a company he was familiar with, nor did he know
much about Jake Taylor; the sensible course was to check
out Jake's financial position—after all there were a lot
of time-wasters in the housing market. Lexi reluctantly
bowed to his superior judgement, while not for one
moment doubting Jake.

How could she, when they had spent a wonderful
Sunday together and she was expecting him back again
on Monday?

At the sound of the car drawing up Lexi dashed out
of the front door to welcome Jake. Her step faltered
when she saw he was not alone. A stunning brunette was
hanging on to his arm. He introduced her as Lorraine,
his PA and right-hand man, but Lexi saw the possessive
gleam in the other woman's eyes, and her heart plum-
meted in her breast. But she need not have worried...

Jake, accurately reading her mind, shrugged off
Lorraine's hand and, stepping forward, pulled Lexi into
his arms and kissed her thoroughly, then whispered, a
hint of laughter in his deep voice, 'Strictly an employee,
little one; you're the only woman for me, understand?'
And she did...

Lexi turned a beaming smile on the other woman, and
quite happily fell in with Jake's suggestion that she show
Lorraine around while he made a couple of phone calls;
he would catch them up in a few minutes.

Leading Lorraine from one room to the next, Lexi,
her jealous fear dispelled, chattered on quite freely, vir-

tually giving Lorraine her life history, and learning in return that the other woman had known Jake from school and had worked for him almost six years. By the time they were viewing the bedrooms, Lexi was feeling quite at ease with the other woman.

'This is a lovely house, and I can see why Jake is interested. But I'm surprised you want to sell it.' Lorraine offered a question in her tone.

'I don't, not really.' Lexi grinned back at her. 'But unless I marry a millionaire real quick I have no choice,' she joked, but she did not see the contemptuous glint in Lorraine's eyes as she led her back out into the hall and down the grand staircase.

'You never considered working, but then your sort never do, born with a silver spoon in your mouth.'

Lexi's head swung around in surprise at the sneering resentment in Lorraine's voice, but before she could answer Jake was with them. The conversation became general, and she put the unsettling comment from her mind.

She was reminded of it abruptly a week later. The next weekend Jake asked her to marry him and Lexi ecstatically accepted. Only to have Lorraine telephone her on the Monday as soon as she heard the news.

'You think you're clever Miss Laughton. "Marry a millionaire real quick," you said. But I've heard of your solicitor Mr Travis's enquiries, and when I tell Jake everything he will be far from pleased. No one has ever questioned Jake Taylor's financial viability; the last thing he needs is his merchant bank asking questions because some gold-digging little hick from the sticks is looking for a wealthy husband. I wouldn't count on marrying him if I were you.'

Lexi did not know what she said in reply—she was too shocked at the other woman's allegations. But she could not deny she had jokingly made the comment about marrying a millionaire. Later, when Lexi repeated

the conversation to Jake and explained about her teasing
comment, he dismissed her fear, saying that he understood Lorraine! She had a chip on her shoulder due to
her upbringing along with a suspicious nature, but there
was no way she would ever convince him that Lexi was
anything other than a beautiful, pure young woman who
had agreed to be his wife. After reinforcing his opinion
with a long, sweet kiss he added that Lorraine was a
great PA—loyal to a fault, but a bit over-protective where
his business interests were concerned. As for Mr Travis
checking his credit rating, it was no more than any efficient lawyer would do for his client, and she was not
to worry; nothing could prevent their marriage.

They were married in a civil ceremony at the register
office in York, three weeks from the day they met, and
flew off to Paris for a brief honeymoon.

Lexi stirred restlessly in the narrow hospital bed. It
had been so beautiful. August in Paris—sparkling blue
skies, and by night, dinner at Maxim's and back to an
exquisite little hotel overlooking the river Seine and
Notre-Dame.

Jake laughingly carried her over the threshold of the
suite and slid her gently to her feet. 'Ready for our dirty
weekend, Miss Laughton?' he teased, as he kicked the
door closed behind him. Lexi smiled and laughed with
him.

They had arrived at Heathrow airport and Jake had
presented the tickets to the check-in clerk, to be informed that Lexi's passport was in the name of Miss
Laughton, while the tickets were in the names of Mrs
and Mrs Taylor. The only way she had been allowed on
the plane was by Jake changing her ticket back into her
maiden name. Jake had thought it was a huge joke, but
Lexi had cringed with embarrassment, even more so
when Jake had handed the passports to the hotel receptionist, while taking the key for the honeymoon suite.
She was sure everyone must think she was a woman of

easy virtue. Jake had howled with laughter and called her old-fashioned.

'The first thing I'm going to do when we get back is change my passport,' Lexi said with a chuckle. Later she was to be glad she didn't...

Jake gathered her into his arms, and with a husky growl declared, 'At last you are mine, and mine alone for always, my beautiful, gorgeous girl. My wife.' She knew no document could bind her more surely to her husband than the love she felt for him.

With gentle hands he removed the turquoise silk dress she wore, sliding it down over her hips to pool in a pale cloud at her feet, all the while pressing tiny kisses to her eyes, her face, her throat.

Sighing, she wrapped her slender arms around his broad shoulders, quivers of sensation darting through her body as she melted helplessly in his hold. He was her husband, her love, and she wanted him with every fibre of her being.

Tenderly, he swung her into his arms and carried her from the sitting-room to the bedroom and carefully laid her down on the huge, old-fashioned four-poster bed. She stared up at him, her love and longing highlighting the pure beauty of her fine features.

Jake, his blue eyes darkened to almost black, reverently bent over her and removed the slight wisps of lace that passed as her underwear and she felt her whole body blush, suddenly overcome with shyness and an unexpected, virginal fear.

'You're my wife, my love; I will never hurt you, I promise,' Jake said throatily, while he quickly divested himself of his clothes.

A gasp of sheer female appreciation escaped Lexi's softly parted lips. Jake was magnificent; she couldn't help staring. His broad shoulders gleamed like polished mahogany in the dim light of the bedside lamp, the musculature of his chest was somehow exaggerated by the downy covering of black hair that arrowed down over his flat stomach to brush out at the apex of his thighs. Her blush deepened as she realised he was fully aroused. She closed her eyes, and felt his lips brush across her mouth.

'Don't be afraid.' He kissed her long and slow. 'Trust me, my darling.' And she did, as his long body covered hers.

When he finally took possession of her pulsating form with one quick thrust, a brief pain was swiftly overtaken by sheer ecstasy. 'Jake.' She cried his name, and her love for him, as they reached the pinnacle together as one. Afterwards, Jake murmured husky rasping avowals of love as he buried his face in her throat...

Slowly, she opened her eyes, a soft sensuous smile curving her lips 'Jake.' Her violet eyes, the lingering traces of sensuality clearly visible, fastened on the dark face looming above her. She stretched up a small hand, and then blinked. He was wearing a sweater... She closed her eyes for a second and it all came flooding back. Jake was sitting on the side of her bed. She was in hospital. The smile vanished from her face. Her baby gone...

'Lexi, are you all right?'

'Yes, yes, I'm fine. I was asleep,' she murmured and, pulling herself up the bed, she sat up.

'Lorraine sends her apologies,' Jake said abruptly. 'Apparently she took the message last night when Stewart and I were in the study. She forgot to tell me afterwards with the pressure of discussing some——' he hesitated, his mouth twisting grimly '—slight alterations Mr Stewart suggested. I know I should fire her for it, and I will if you say so. But I feel it was partly my fault. The discussion became quite heated, and Lorraine isn't like other women. She would never forget a business message, but anything else she doesn't see as important.'

'Don't fire her for my sake, Jake,' Lexi responded quietly. She knew Lorraine did not like her, hadn't from the beginning when she'd tried to convince Jake that Lexi was only after his money and that he was making a mistake in marrying her. 'Tell her I accept her apology.' She looked up and saw Jake was looking somewhere over her left shoulder, his expression oddly evasive, and she wondered, not for the first time, just what relationship Jake had with his PA.

'You're very generous, Lexi. I've done some investigating today and I should have asked about the baby last night, when I phoned, but I assumed it was all right, while the young nurse I spoke to assumed I already knew you had lost it.'

'It.' He called their baby 'it'. How could he be so insensitive? '*It* doesn't matter, as long as your business was successful, all is not lost,' she said with a biting sarcasm that was wasted as Jake glanced down, and leaning forward, kissed her lightly on the lips.

'Thank you, Lexi, you're very forgiving. I want you to get better and come home. I miss you.' His dark eyes searched her still pale face. 'Everything will be fine, I promise.' And, lifting one long finger, trailed it down her cheek. 'How about a smile, hmm?'

'I'll be coming home tomorrow,' she offered with a pitiful attempt at a smile.

'Good, and perhaps now you can return to London and college, if you like.'

Lexi felt like screaming. When they were first married they had lived in London and Jake had suggested she stay at home, saying she had no need for a degree in languages, he would give her a degree in love instead. Many a lunchtime he dashed back to the apartment and they spent hours in bed. Or they drove up to Yorkshire to oversee the renovations on the manor. Then, when the hotel had been completed by the Easter, they moved permanently to Yorkshire, Jake saying he could work as easily from his study in the apartment. Lorraine could look after the London office. The new apartment was a delight, and Lexi had quite happily spent the past months helping out in the hotel reception.

But had she been happy, she suddenly questioned, or had the feeling of resentment towards Jake started long before she lost the baby? When only weeks after having her pregnancy confirmed Jake suddenly, because of 'pressure of business' he had said, took to spending all week in London, returning to Yorkshire only at the weekends, while insisting she stay in the country; it was better for her, he had said, as a mum-to-be.

Now Jake was calmly suggesting she go back to London and college as though nothing had happened.

She hid her anger and resentment as he arranged to collect her the next day and kissed her goodbye. But after he had left it hit her. Jake had avoided telling her whether his deal of the previous night was successful or not. But then he had been very evasive the last few weeks about his business; no doubt Lorraine would know!

Lexi wondered yet again how close her husband and Lorraine were. On their honeymoon Lexi had asked Jake if he had ever had an affair with his PA and Jake had said 'Good God, no!' and burst out laughing, but Lexi had never been able to see the joke...

CHAPTER TWO

LEXI, dressed in the same blue jeans and soft T-shirt she had worn on Friday before her accident, was sitting on the edge of the hospital bed waiting for her husband. The necessary discharge papers had been signed an hour ago. She glanced out of the window for the hundredth time; the sun was rising high in the sky, embracing the utilitarian lines of the hospital building in a rosy glow, but its warmth could not pierce the coldness in Lexi's heart.

Jake entered the room in a rush, full of apologies for the delay. 'Sorry, darling, Lorraine and I were tied up on a conference call. You would not believe the inefficiency of the telecommunications here. We were disconnected half a dozen times.' He frowned. 'In today's climate of recession, speed and efficiency are essential to sustain success.'

Did it matter? she wondered bleakly as five minutes later she was comfortably seated in Jake's car as he eased it out of the hospital gates.

'Lorraine has arranged for Meg to come in every day for the next week or two.' He shot her a quick sideways glance. 'I don't want you doing anything at all until you are completely recovered.'

Lorraine seemed to be arranging an awful lot in her life lately, Lexi thought bitterly, and was stung into replying, 'She needn't have bothered. What is there to recover from? I've had a miscarriage, not lost a limb. In fact, the quicker I can get back into Reception and working, the better I'll like it.' Lexi knew she was being deliberately antagonistic, but she couldn't help it. It was either anger or tears, and she had cried enough to last a lifetime.

'Lexi, please. Lorraine was only trying to help, to make up for forgetting the message the other night. You're in shock, you need...'

'Jake,' she cut in, 'I know what I need and it is to get back to normal as quickly as possible. So please, just leave me alone.' And she wished flaming Lorraine would vanish in a puff of smoke...

The car came to an abrupt halt outside the entrance to their private wing. Jake turned towards her, his eyes narrowed faintly as they took in her pale, determined expression. 'You need a rest.' And before she could protest he had lifted her from the car and carried her into the house and up to their bedroom, and laid her gently on the bed.

'The doctor told me to be prepared for rapid mood swings, darling, and you can complain as much as you like but you will do as I say,' he commanded arrogantly, and then he leant over her and brushed his lips along her brow. 'Is there anything you want?'

Her baby back... but the words were never said as, wretched, she flopped back against the pillow, listless and lifeless. A faint sigh left her lips. 'No, I'm fine. I'll join you downstairs later.'

'Good girl.' He straightened, his dark eyes smiling compassionately down at her. 'We will have other children, Lexi. We have plenty of time.'

She managed a weak smile, but, for the first time since meeting Jake, she was actually relieved to see him leave the room.

Meg, bless her, was all sympathy with Lexi as she woke her with a cup of tea and the information that dinner was almost ready. Lexi smiled weakly at the small, grey-haired woman who had been the daily at Forest Manor as long as she could remember.

'Nothing ever seems to work right for me in this house, does it, Meg? My mother died here, my father, and now my baby. Maybe if I had stayed in London and never come back here I wouldn't have lost my baby.'

'Don't be ridiculous,' Meg said shortly. 'Losing a baby has nothing to do with where one lives. You're just clutching at straws, my girl. Now come on, up, dressed, and down, and look after that husband of yours. We don't want that black-eyed witch latching on to him, now, do we?'

Lexi chuckled. Meg's opinion of Jake's PA was on a par with her own. The woman might be tall and sophisticated and a brilliant businesswoman, but she gave Lexi the creeps, and, even though Jake denied any involvement with her, Lexi had a suspicion that it wasn't for the want of trying by Lorraine...

Sitting at the dinner-table half an hour later with Jake and Lorraine was hardly a relaxing experience. Although Jake made a great effort to keep the conversation flowing, Lexi found it increasingly difficult to answer in anything but monosyllables, until the other two began discussing a Docklands development Jake was involved in, and Lexi was no longer required to speak at all.

Lorraine, as if forgetting Lexi's presence altogether, became quite explicit. 'Really, Jake, you have to decide if you want the deal and go for it. A conference call is not going to do the trick. You'll have to be in London tomorrow at the latest.'

'Not now, Lorraine.' Jake said curtly, shooting the dark woman a warning glance, and, turning to Lexi, added, 'I'm staying here. Don't worry, darling.'

'Please, Jake,' Lexi pleaded softly, she could sense the undercurrent in the air there was something going on she knew nothing about, and right at the moment she did not care. 'I'll be OK with Meg, in fact I think I would like to be on my own for a while. If you're needed in London I really think you should go.'

'No way.' He reached across the table and caught her small hand in his. 'You need me.'

The tenderness in his gaze was almost Lexi's undoing, her lips began to tremble but with a great effort of will she pulled her hand free. 'I'd rather you went, honestly, Jake.'

'That's settled, then.' Lorraine spoke up. 'You're being over-protective, Jake. I'll get back to London after dinner and set up a meeting for tomorrow.'

Jake's dark eyes caught Lexi's, a query in their depths. 'You've had a very traumatic emotional experience; you need my support.'

His support was a little late in coming, Lexi thought bitterly. He had barely mentioned their child. It had been a boy. Did Jake know that? She had no idea. The same as she had no idea what perverse sense of justice was motivating her angry resentment.

Lexi looked into her husband's dark, serious face and wanted to reach out to him and beg him to stay, hold her, comfort her, but somewhere deep inside she felt an aching guilt. It was her fault she had lost their baby; she did not deserve the tender loving care in his eyes; she had failed him in the one thing a woman should give her husband, and, because of that, the very least she could do by recompense was not get in the way of his business. She glanced across at Lorraine and saw the impatience in the other woman's eyes.

'Really, Jake. Lexi has only had a miscarriage. It happens to women every day and they get over it. In fact, it might be a blessing in disguise. We are going to be frightfully busy over the next few months. You wouldn't have much time for a child just now. Next year would be much better.'

Lexi couldn't believe the insensitivity of Lorraine, but she did catch a glimpse of something that looked very much like relief in her husband's eyes, just before he exploded.

'For God's sake, Lorraine. Keep your bloody opinions to yourself,' Jake swore violently. 'You might be a brilliant businesswoman, but in the feminine stakes we both know you're a non-starter. Can't you see you're upsetting Lexi? How can you be so heartless? It was my child as well...'

'Sorry-y.' Lorraine drawled and, pushing back her chair left the table. 'If I'm driving back to London tonight, I'd better get started. Give me a ring at home later and tell me what you decide.' And she left the room.

Lexi, with head bowed, pushed the remains of her chicken chasseur around her plate, too choked to speak. She felt a hard hand curve around her shoulder and looked up. Jake had walked around behind her and was leaning over her.

'I'm sorry, Lexi. Ignore Lorraine. She's a great PA but home and family are of no importance to her. She doesn't mean to be callous, she just doesn't think unless it is business... Come on, I'll take you back upstairs.'

'I can manage on my own.'

'I know, darling, but indulge me, hmmm?' And lifting her to her feet he swung her up into his strong arms, his deep blue eyes riveted on her own. 'I don't like feeling helpless, Lexi, and losing our baby has left me that way.'

She felt the tears fill her eyes. Jake was hurting just the same as her, and she made no demur when he carried her back to the bedroom.

Gently he let her slide down the long length of him, linking his arms behind her back and holding her steady against his hard body for a long moment. She let her head drop against his chest and felt the firm, steady beat of his heart beneath her cheek, and found it oddly reassuring.

'I'll always be here for you, Lexi, you know that, don't you?'

She raised her face to his. 'Yes. Yes, I know, but Lorraine is right. I'll be fine; your business is important in London, please go.' And, forcing a smile to her soft lips, she teased, 'After all, you will only be a telephone call away, and surely British Telecom can get a single call right.'

'Shhh, sweetheart, I'm not going anywhere.' His dark head swooped and his firm lips covered hers in a gentle kiss. 'Everything will work out,' he murmured against her mouth. 'But now get into bed, and rest. I'll join you later.'

Lexi turned away and, slipping out of her clothes, she headed for the bathroom. Everything would work out. Jake had said so... but somehow, for the first time since her marriage, she wasn't quite so sure.

A couple of hours later, Lexi woke from a light, troubled doze to the sight of Jake striding across the room from the bathroom, completely naked. Her violet eyes slid over his hard-muscled body almost with dislike. He was perfect, so alive, all virile male, but her son was dead and she felt a failure.

When he slid into bed beside her and drew her into his arms, she didn't offer any resistance, needing his protective embrace, until she realised, with something very like disgust as he folded her into the heat of his body, a hard thigh over her slender limbs, that he was sexually aroused. She pushed him away with an angry snort. 'My God, Jake. How can you?'

'Hush, Lexi, I don't want to do anything, just hold you, but you know you always have this effect on me. You don't have to do anything: a look, a smile, you just have to be there and my body reacts... and it has been a few empty nights without you,' he drawled softly, adding, 'Just lie still and soon I'll relax.'

She tilted her small head back and looked up into his shadowy features, barely visible in the moon's silvery light beaming through the window. His dark eyes burned down into hers, a sensual, teasing gleam in their indigo depths. 'Unless, of course, you want to help me relax,' he murmured throatily, kissing her softly parted lips.

She knew exactly what he meant; until she had become pregnant they had enjoyed a full, totally erotic sensual relationship. He had taught her everything she knew about sex and also how to please him, but in the circumstances she found it distasteful, and, pushing herself out of his arms, she slid to the far side of the bed.

'My God! Surely you can control your insatiable appetite for once? You disgust me.' She felt the instant tension in his large body at her words but she didn't care if she had hurt him. She was hurting too much herself.

'I was only teasing, Lexi, trying to cheer you up. This is as hard for me as it is for you, darling, and I don't know how to handle it.'

'Try using the spare bedroom,' she said curtly. 'I need my sleep.'

'Do you mean that?' He sat up in bed, his hands grasping her slender shoulders and pinning her to the bed. 'Is that really what you want? You know I'll do anything to make it easier for you.'

It wasn't what she wanted; she wanted to be held in his arms and sleep with her head on his chest, have him tell her how much he loved her, tell her it wasn't her fault they had lost the baby, but she couldn't say any of those things. Instead, in a small, tight voice, she looked straight up into his puzzled eyes and said, 'Yes, I would prefer to be alone, if you don't mind.' She noticed the flash of pain in his expression before he quickly controlled it.

'Dr Bell said to pamper you, so all right.' His dark head lowered and she knew he was going to kiss her but deliberately she turned her head away and his lips brushed her cheek. 'Goodnight, darling,' he said softly. She felt him leave the bed and a few seconds' silence before the door closed with a soft thump.

What had she done? And why? She didn't know. The huge bed was lonely without Jake, and slowly the tears trickled down her cheeks. She didn't recognise the person she had become, and, as she sank into an exhausted sleep, her tired mind gave up trying to find an answer.

Over the next few weeks, Lexi seemed to move through the days in a world of her own. Oh, she functioned all right on a purely practical level, but on an emotional level she was numb, haunted by guilt because she had lost the child. Not even Jake could get through to her.

The first morning back at Forest Manor, he had been all concern, refusing to leave for London, until on the Wednesday evening he insisted on taking her out to dinner, trying to cheer her up. They dined at Number 19 Grape Lane in York, the first place they had ever shared a meal together, but the exquisite food tasted like sawdust in her mouth, and she heaved a sigh of relief when Jake finally suggested returning home.

As she slipped her nightdress over her head, a soft confection of satin and lace, Jake walked into the bedroom. She lifted her head, and eyed him across the wide expanse of the large bed. He was fresh from the shower, his dark hair slicked back across his proud head, his body gleaming golden, naked except for a short white towel slung around his hips, his long sinewy legs planted slightly apart. He looked like every woman's dream of a lover, but to Lexi he appeared as a threat to her blessed numb state. She watched wary-eyed as he walked around the bed to stand in front of her.

His strong hands curved around her upper arms and he eased her towards him. 'Lexi, we have to talk. You've slept alone long enough; it's becoming a habit.'

She tensed her body rigid in his hold.

'Don't get me wrong, sweetheart. I know it is too soon for lovemaking.'

'How thoughtful,' she snapped curtly.

'Give me some credit, Lexi, but you have to understand, separate beds are not the answer to your problem.
You need care and comfort.' His dark head bent towards
her.

'Not now,' she said starkly, and watched as Jake's
proud head reared back.

'Then when, Lexi? You hardly talk any more.'

'I do, I worked in Reception today for a couple of
hours, and thoroughly enjoyed it.' And she had. Jake
had been working in his study and she had walked
through to the hotel just as a party of French tourists
arrived. She had felt quite animated for a while, getting
back to work.

'You can talk to strangers, but not to your husband?'
he queried silkily, his mask of concern slipping to reveal
his frustration. 'For God's sake, Lexi, you have to snap
out of it.' His fingers dug into her flesh and she winced,
her head lifting fractionally in time to catch the flare of
frightening anger in his dark eyes, quickly controlled.

'It's hard, I know, Lexi, but we have to try and forget.
When I first met you the one thing I noticed, above your
beauty and your voluptuous little body——' his dark eyes
swept lingeringly over her from head to toe and then
back to her upturned face '—was your eager appetite
for life, your vibrancy; don't let this one set-back knock
all the life out of you. I want my wife back as she was.
I want us to get back to normal as quickly as possible,'
he declared frustratedly.

'If what you say is true,' she opined with remarkable
calm, considering his naked chest was scraping gently
against the delicate fabric of her nightgown over her
softly rounded breasts, 'I think you should return to
London tomorrow. After all, for the past couple of
months you've worked in the city all week, only returning home at weekends. That's normal for us.' Her
huge violet eyes held his gaze and she watched his eyes
darken almost to jet, feeling the tension in his hard body.

She thought she heard him murmur, 'I need you,' but she must have been mistaken as, with a faint sigh, Jake slid his hands up her throat and cupped her small face.

'Yes, whatever you want.' And, holding her head steady, he closed his firm, sensuous mouth over hers in a hard, possessive kiss. He straightened abruptly. 'And God knows the business certainly needs me, even if you don't.' And he left, a defeated slant to his broad shoulders.

After that night, Jake returned to the London apartment and his head office, and Lexi slipped into a regular routine: she worked a few hours every day in Reception, and at weekends Jake returned home.

He took her out for dinner, and to the theatre in York; he even insisted on them spending a day at Castle Howard, but nothing could snap her out of her lethargy, and the separate bedrooms remained... Meg tried as well, warning her that she was a fool to leave her husband alone with the lovely Lorraine all week—she was just asking for trouble. But Lexi refused to listen. If Jake slept with Lorraine, it was no more than she had always suspected, she told herself, and refused to admit there was anything wrong.

She worked, didn't she? So what if she was a bit quiet? Surely it was allowed after all she had suffered. And she wrapped her grief around her like a shroud.

Lexi opened her eyes slowly and turned over in the large bed, just for a second she felt a pang of something like regret that Jake's hard masculine body wasn't there beside her. She sighed deeply and, pushing the tangled mass of her flame-coloured hair from her small face, she stretched and sat up. She looked around the room. A few short months ago, when the renovations were first finished, this room had been her pride and joy; she had chosen the decoration, a soft blend of peaches and cream saved from being too feminine by the heavy antique mahogany furniture. The summer sun streamed through the window, dancing into every little nook and cranny. It was a gorgeous summer day, and then she remembered the date—it was a Wednesday, her day for a check-up with Dr Bell, but also it was the day before her first wedding anniversary.

Dr Bell took one look at her and demanded to know what was wrong. Lexi broke down and told him: her guilt over losing the baby, her distaste for sex, even her suspicion that Jake was having an affair with Lorraine. Three hours later, after much good advice, such as 'try taking a holiday', Lexi found herself sitting on the afternoon train heading for London, and Jake.

She watched the patchwork of the countryside sliding past the carriage window in the hot summer sun and she felt as if she had awakened from a long sleep. Not so much sleep as nightmare, she admitted ruefully. Dear Dr Bell had explained everything: she had been suffering from hormonal depression and the fact that she had lost the baby and was consumed with guilt about it had made her worse, prone to suspicion, irrational... But once the doctor had convinced her it was a quite common reaction to a miscarriage, she had suddenly felt rejuvenated.

Lexi had taken great care with her appearance, for the first time in weeks. Her red hair shone like living flame and cascaded down her back in lavish curls. The smart, sleeveless plain mint-green silk sheath she wore clung lovingly to her slender curves and ended just above her knees, revealing a goodly amount of shapely legs; on her feet she wore high-heeled white pumps and she carried a small white clutch bag in her hand containing her passport. A hastily packed suitcase was on the rack above her head. She was going to surprise Jake, and persuade him to let his super-efficient Lorraine look after the business while he accompanied Lexi to Paris for the rest of the week, a repetition of their honeymoon a year ago. It would be perfect . . .

The first hint that Lexi's plan was not going to go smoothly came as the train ground to a halt, half an hour away from King's Cross station. Lexi heard with dismay that the train was delayed because of a bomb scare at the station, and to make matters worse a glance out of the carriage window showed the blue sky turn to black and the heavens open in a storm that would have rivalled Noah's. She consulted the slim gold watch on her wrist and sighed. She would not catch him at the office, but still, she told herself, it didn't matter. She would catch him at the apartment; they had spent many a happy hour there when they were first married.

Dreamily she recalled the first weeks when they were so close. Jake had told her all about himself. He was a self-made man, and a bastard, he had declared on their second date, but luckier than most. Apparently, his mother had fallen in love with a married man when on holiday on the continent, and Jake was the result. The married man, to give him his due, had provided for the mother and child. He had paid for a Victorian terraced house in London for them, and every month a cheque arrived, though the man himself never put in an appearance. When Jake was sixteen the money had stopped coming, and they had only been able to assume the man had died. Jake had left school and begun working on building sites and, after the death of his mother four years later, he had taken his first step into the business world, by converting the three-storey house into apartments.

Lexi smiled reminiscently; they had been lying naked in bed in their Paris hotel and she had teased him about being a self-made millionaire at thirty. Laughingly he had responded, 'If you married me for money, as Lorraine would have me believe, you're in for a shock. Every penny I make I reinvest; a paper millionaire need not necessarily have spare cash floating around. But don't worry, I won't see you go hungry.' And, leaning over her satiated naked body, he had murmured throatily, 'Take a bite of me any time, darling.'

The train started with a jolt, jerking Lexi out of her reverie; she was surprised to note they had been delayed well over an hour. Still, soon she would see her husband, and she hugged the thought to her with secret delight.

Before getting a taxi from the station she took time to purchase from one of the small boutiques a bottle of Jake's favourite aftershave. Kindly the assistant gift-wrapped it for her. Not a very exciting or original anniversary present, but the best she could do at short notice. Ten minutes later, she was sitting in the back of a taxi speeding through the streets of London.

With a light step she dashed across the pavement and into the entrance of the mansion block that housed Jake's apartment, dodging the sheeting rain. The lovely summer day had deteriorated into a very wet and windy night. Still, nothing could dampen her spirits and, with suitcase in one hand and bag and gift in the other, she dashed up the flight of stairs to the first-floor apartment.

She placed her suitcase on the floor and, taking her key from her bag, let herself into the cosy flat. A short hall with a telephone table and cloak cupboard was thickly carpeted in a deep, dark red. Silently she moved along the hall; she stopped at the hall table and deposited the parcel on it and the suitcase at her feet, and then took a step further to the living-room door. She reached out to open it but it was not closed and swung half-open at her touch, and then she froze.

Jake was already at home, and not alone. A small balcony with various large green houseplants partly obscured the door from the two people sitting side by side on a large, curved, black hide sofa in the sunken lounge. But Lexi could see all too clearly. Jake and Lorraine, a bottle of wine, and two glasses on the table beside them, but, more damning than that, they were both wearing only towelling robes.

She stood numb with shock, the rainwater dripping from her long hair, running icily down her spine, her thin dress no match for the storm outside. But the storm in her heart was worse. She listened in open-mouthed horror as her life dissolved around her.

'It's no good, Lorraine, I just can't tell Lexi. At least not yet. She's just lost a child, for God's sake! She will be so hurt...' Jake's deep voice sounded harsh in the stillness of the room.

'You're being ridiculous, Jake. She has to know some time and if you don't tell her she'll find out anyway, and that will hurt her a hell of a lot more. It is impossible to keep a thing like this secret.' Her scarlet-tipped nails reached out and curved around Jake's arm, and Lexi, from her vantage place at the door, flinched as though she had been struck.

'I've told you before, Jake, you're far too protective of Lexi. She is a twenty-year-old woman, she has lost a child; she knows the world is not all sweetness and light. These things happen and there's nothing anyone can do about it. You cut your losses, and try again.'

'You don't understand, Lorraine. I made a promise to Lexi when I married her. What am I supposed to say to her? "Sorry, darling, but circumstances have changed, and it's a tough old world out there. Sorry I've got to break my word, but I'm sure you understand..."' he drawled sarcastically.

'She will understand, Jake, and it's not as if you're leaving her with nothing; she's a sleeping partner in the business—half of all you make is hers. Personally, I always thought she was a gold-digger anyway. I told you so when you insisted on marrying her. She might jump at the chance of being rich in her own right...I know if I was in her position I would.'

'Lexi has been protected all her life; she's not like you.' Jake's dark head turned to the woman at his side. 'That's why you make such a damn good PA: you're as tough as any man and mercenary to boot, but fortunately Lexi is not.'

Lexi had seen and heard enough. 'It's not as if you're leaving her with nothing,' echoed in her head. How could she have been such a fool? Her husband and his PA were having an affair; they were actually discussing how he was to divorce her. For all Lexi knew it had been going on since long before she had met Jake. Suddenly it was blatantly obvious, she realised with numb acceptance. Jake had only married her for Forest Manor.

She recalled their wedding-day, when she had mentioned eventually settling at Forest Manor and Jake's look of shocked surprise. She had naïvely assumed, with their marriage and Jake's promise to pay her father's debts, that the house would stay a house. But Jake had quickly put her straight. It was still essential that the place be turned into a hotel, though he did promise they could keep a private wing for themselves. Lexi, so in love, had of course agreed.

So many little things suddenly made sense. At first, when the hotel was completed, Jake had insisted he could work as easily in Yorkshire as London. But almost as soon as her pregnancy was confirmed suddenly business was hard and he needed to be in London all week. Now she realised Jake must have wanted out of the marriage from the minute the hotel was up and running and making money for him. No wonder the pair sitting on the sofa before her had been so negative about Lexi's pregnancy. While she was devastated at the loss of her child, her swine of a husband had probably been laughing with relief. It was this thought more than anything that gave Lexi the strength to do what she did next.

Straightening her shoulders, she walked out on to the small balcony but did not descend the steps to the couple below. Standing above them gave her some sense of superiority, even if it was just an illusion.

Jake saw her first and jumped to his feet, swinging around to look up at her. 'Lexi, what are you doing here?' His dark face was flushed, and for once he looked less than in complete control as his strong hands tugged at the belt around his waist holding his robe together.

Lexi's violet eyes narrowed to mere slits of purple ice. 'I called to tell you I'm going on a little holiday with Cathy, a friend from school, but I couldn't help overhearing your conversation.' By this time Lorraine had stood up next to Jake. Lexi almost choked. The woman was wearing Lexi's robe, and it was too small for her, or perhaps, from a man's point of view, it was perfect, barely covering the other woman's large breasts.

'Lexi, let me explain.' Jake moved towards the stairs.

Imperviously, Lexi held up her small hand. 'There is really no need, Jake. I heard everything, and I hate to disillusion you, but you are wrong about me, and Lorraine was right. I really don't care about you breaking your promise to me. I would much rather have the money.' If Lexi had any lingering doubt about the perfidiousness of Jake it vanished, as she recognised the look of pure undisguised relief that spread over his handsome face.

'You heard it all, everything, and you really don't mind...?' He smiled up at her. 'Thank God for that! I was dreading telling you. You've been so down lately, losing the child and everything; I just never imagined you would be so sensible. I think this calls for a drink. Champagne even.' And holding up a hand to her he said, 'Come on down, and we can all celebrate.'

Celebrate! The heartless swine, but then, why was she surprised? She had never been a match for the sophisticated couple in front of her, and perhaps in her heart of hearts she had always known that. Only once had she mentioned to Jake that he seemed very close to his PA and he had burst out laughing, though he was flattered that Lexi was jealous. The bastard! She swore under her breath, but not by a flicker of an eyelid did she reveal her true feelings; instead she responded smoothly, 'I'm afraid I haven't time, the taxi is waiting downstairs...'

In three steps Jake was beside her. 'Don't be ridiculous. You can't leave just like that! Lexi, I knew nothing about you taking a holiday.' His strong hands reached out for her but she took a hasty step back into the hall, she grabbed her suitcase and headed for the door. Jake caught her as she opened the door.

'Wait, Lexi, I refuse to let you go off like this; we have things to discuss,' he declared adamantly. 'You've been ill, for God's sake!'

'You have no say in the matter any more. You broke your promise, and now I'm breaking mine. Go back and celebrate with Lorraine.' Her face a cold mask, she stared straight at him. 'As for me, I never want to see you again.'

If she had slapped him, she couldn't have shocked him more. His hand fell from her arm and all the colour drained out of his face. 'You don't mean that, Lexi, you're being childish. I thought you said you understood... Sit down, have a drink and...

'Call my solicitor in York with the divorce papers,' she cut him off, and spun around.

'My God! You don't care, not for me, the hotel...Lorraine was right all along, you mercenary little bitch...'

But Lexi barely heard him. She was free, out of the door, and running down the staircase, her suitcase banging against her leg as she moved and the tears streaming down her face. She vaguely heard Jake's harsh voice shouting after her but she did not stop running until she had put a couple of streets between herself and her louse of a husband.

Finally she waved down a cab and collapsed in the back seat. 'Just drive around, please,' she murmured.

'You're the boss,' the driver said flatly.

The tears dried on her face, her violet eyes huge and blankly staring inward... 'Childish,' Jake had called her for not accepting that he wanted to divorce her with the sophisticated *élan* he expected from his women.

Hormonal depression, she thought with dry irony, What a joke! Deep in her subconscious, hadn't she always wondered what the dynamic London businessman saw in her? Why a man of Jake's obvious wealth and charm would marry a naïve young woman from Yorkshire? She had always sensed the ruthless streak in him but had convinced herself it would never be turned on her. Jake loved her! And that was the biggest joke of all. He had swept her off her feet, used her body in lust, and even that hadn't satisfied him for long.

She groaned, a small whimper of sound. All her suspicions about Jake and Lorraine had been confirmed in one horrendous evening. Jake had probably been making love to Lorraine every time he was in London, while Lexi, as the little wife, was in happy ignorance, working in the hotel miles away. Lexi closed her eyes briefly to shut out the pain; she would not give in to it, she vowed silently.

Dear heaven! While she was losing her child Jake and Lorraine had most likely been in each other's arms... She couldn't bear to think about it, and, opening her eyes, her mouth a tight white line, she made a silent promise. Jake had hurt her for the last time...

Her mind was made up. She had used her old school chum's name on the spur of the moment earlier, but actually it was a good idea. The thought of Cathy was comforting. They were both children of diplomats and had spent five years together at the same convent school in Sussex. They had shared a flat in London for a year but had not been in touch since Lexi had dropped out of college. But Lexi was pretty sure Cathy still had the same apartment. She gave the cabbie her friend's address, and half an hour later Lexi was being warmly welcomed by an amazon of a girl with green hair into an Earl's Court apartment that looked like a bomb had hit it.

'Hey, you hardly look the happy mum-to-be. What's happened?'

Lexi collapsed on the beaten-up sofa, and between her tears told Cathy everything...

The following day she made a long phone call to her solicitor in York, advising him that soon he would be receiving divorce papers from her husband, and instructing him to act on her behalf, to accept whatever Jake said without query, but on no account to let her husband have the new address she would forward to Mr Travis as soon as she was settled.

With the old man's condolences ringing in her ears she replaced the receiver, and, with a grim smile for Cathy, said, 'Right, to your parents', and then as far away from England as I can get, and if by any remote chance you bump into Jake Taylor you have never seen me, and have no idea where I am. Promise...' And Cathy did.

CHAPTER THREE

LEXI stepped out of the lift at the ground floor, her glance sweeping professionally around the elegant marble foyer, lingering slightly on the view of the dining-room through large double doors. Yes, all was serene; the few guests who had opted to lunch in the hotel were being attended to with the expert efficiency expected of the staff at the Hotel Le Piccolo Paradiso.

As manager of the small, exclusive hotel it was Lexi's job to make sure everything ran smoothly, and even now, when she was off duty and on her way down into Sorrento for the rest of the day, she could not help checking everything was in order.

Today it was slightly more than that, she admitted to herself with a wry smile. She was meeting Dante for lunch and he would be expecting to hear if she was going ahead with the divorce. It was still a niggling puzzle to Lexi why Jake Taylor, in almost five years, had never instigated divorce proceedings. It just didn't make sense. The last night in London she had heard Jake and Lorraine discussing how to break the news to his wife of their involvement and they had even got around to discussing the money side of divorce, and wondering if Lexi would accept it. When she had faced Jake he had made no attempt to deny anything, was delighted she had overheard and was going to be sensible and actually suggested she join them in a drink.

For years she had been expecting to hear from Mr Travis, her solicitor, that Jake had approached him for a divorce but it had never happened. When Dante had asked her out a few months ago, she had decided it was time she got back into the world of male-female relationships, and to do so she had to be free. Finally, a week ago she had rung Mr Travis in England and, after a long conversation with the lawyer, she had confirmed in writing her desire to start divorce proceedings on the five years' separation statute. This very morning she had received a letter from her solicitor confirming that the proceedings were progressing on her behalf.

Dismissing the problem from her mind, she strolled over to the reception desk and in her usual fluent Italian asked Franco, her young assistant manager, if everything was in order.

'*Si*, Lexi.' His dark brown eyes swept over her appreciatively, taking in the rich tumble of golden-red curls flowing down her back and the seductive silhouette of her voluptuous figure outlined in a brief blue cotton jersey scooped-neck shift dress. Her shapely legs were bare and golden as was the rest of her exposed flesh. Five years in Sorrento and she had matured into a stunningly beautiful woman from the slim, rather solemn girl who had first arrived. Franco sighed dramatically. 'Meeting Signor Dante? I think he is a very lucky man.'

Lexi grinned in acceptance of the compliment. 'Forever the charmer, Franco,' she quipped. '*Ciao.*' And her strappy blue sandals tapped out her jaunty step as she crossed the marble floor and stepped outside into the brilliant blaze of midsummer sun.

She stopped for a moment beside the little Fiat Panda—it was a company car but Lexi considered it hers—she stared out over the roof of the car at the view before her. It never failed to lift her spirits, she thought musingly. The hotel was perched high on a hill overlooking the bay of Naples. The isle of Capri was visible on the left, an exquisite jewel set in a sea of azure. With a contented sigh, Lexi opened the car door and sat in the driving seat.

Why worry? she told herself. According to the solicitor, in six weeks' time she could divorce Jake Taylor on the grounds that they had been apart for five years; she didn't even need her husband's consent. Dante should be satisfied with that. Very soon she would be officially free...

She started the little car and spun along the elegant drive lined with orange and lemon trees and turned right at the main gates on to the road down into Sorrento. She was singing softly to herself as she swung the wheel expertly around the first of half a dozen hairpin bends that zig-zagged down the hillside, only to gasp as, with lightning speed, a black Bugatti sports car swerved violently to pass her, only missing her car by inches.

The same blasted car again! Stupid macho oaf, she thought scathingly, as she registered the brief outline of a dark, greying man behind the wheel of the gleaming monster of a car. But, once more steadily driving along, she had the same uncomfortable feeling that there was something vaguely familiar about the driver of the Bugatti. She had seen the car a few times in the past few months. It was hard to miss; at first she had thought the driver might have been a guest at some time. But the hotel was small—only twenty luxuriously appointed suites, strictly for the very wealthy and discerning traveller, and she knew virtually all the guests, past and present.

She had never actually got a good look at the driver. But somehow she had the strangest feeling she knew the man on a more personal basis. Which was ridiculous when she thought about it; people with the sort of wealth that could afford a Bugatti were not in her social circle. Dante, her boyfriend, was comfortably off, owning two jewellery shops—one in Sorrento and another in Amalfi. He was a good, hard-working, serious-minded man and would make her an excellent husband and father to her children.

A shadow darkened her violet eyes, as she realised with a sense of shock it would be exactly five years to-night since she had lost her child. She had never completely got over the miscarriage, and sometimes in her darkest moods she couldn't help asking herself if she had finally instigated divorce proceedings herself and was contemplating marrying Dante, more because she still had a desperate longing for a child, than through any great love for the man himself.

She dismissed the unsettling thought from her mind. Anyway, Dante hadn't actually proposed yet, she smiled wryly, counting her chickens again! A bad policy, she remonstrated with herself, as she manoeuvred the car through the hectic lunch-time traffic in Sorrento and down to the Marina Piccolae. She had arranged to meet Dante at the Dolphin restaurant, a long wooden structure that stretched out on wooden stilts from the steep cliffs into the sea and served excellent fish dishes. She parked the car on a small cobbled side-lane and walked around the curve of the old port.

A tender smile curved the corners of her full mouth as she watched the local children playing in the sea. It didn't seem to bother them that there were fishing boats tied up haphazardly around the water's edge; in fact it appeared to add to their enjoyment as, like fish themselves, they jumped and dived off the boats.

Sorrento was a stunning town, built over a flat plateau that rose precipitously from the sea. On the top of the steep cliffs the big hotels had lifts cut through the rock and down to the base and the sea. Small beaches with large rectangular wooden pontoons greatly increased the available sunbathing areas and, for the swimmer, access to the sea itself, but at quite a substantial charge to the public. Certainly more than local children could pay.

Lexi glanced at her watch. Oh, hell! She was late. Putting a spurt on, she dashed the last hundred yards to the restaurant, and breathlessly walked through the dining-room and out on to the open-air deck. She glanced around and smiled as she caught sight of Dante. He had not seen her and for a moment she allowed her gaze to linger on his downbent head. He was such a nice man. At forty-two he was beginning to get a little heavy, maybe, but nothing could take away from his friendly smiling face as he looked up and caught her gaze. Of medium height, with the black curling locks of a true Neapolitan and huge thick-lashed dark brown eyes, he reminded Lexi of some lovely cuddly spaniel.

He stood up as she approached. 'Late again, *cara*.' And holding out her chair for her he brushed her cheek with his lips. 'But you are worth the wait.'

She had not seen him for over a week and his husky compliment did wonders for her self-esteem. She sat down with a contented sigh, and looked out over the sea with complete satisfaction. Yes, she had made the right decision. England had no appeal for her any more. Her life now was in Italy with Dante and in a few weeks she would be free to marry him, and turning her attention to her companion she smiled brilliantly. 'Dante, have I ever told you? You are a truly lovely man.'

His broad, tanned face split in a huge grin. 'In that case, let's eat quick and go back to my place for siesta.'

She chuckled. 'You never miss a chance.'

Suddenly serious, Dante caught her hand in his across the table. 'I don't intend to, I've waited months for you. Have you heard from England?'

Lexi withdrew her hand from his as the waiter arrived with two plates of superbly grilled langoustines in garlic butter. Dante knew her taste so well and had already ordered. 'Yes, yes, I have, and I've checked the law with my solicitor and he has told me that in a few weeks' time, when the separation has lasted five years, I can have a divorce with or without my husband's consent. I got a letter this morning and the wheels have already been set in motion. No problem.'

'You're sure?' he demanded sceptically.

'Absolutely,' she confirmed.

'In that case, how about a November wedding? Most of the tourists have left by then and we can take an extended honeymoon.'

Not the most romantic proposal in the world, she thought, her lips twitching in a wry grin, but in the past few months Dante had let her know in countless ways that marriage was on his mind. Which was why she had finally got the courage to apply for a divorce herself. After all, five years without sight or sound of her husband was enough proof for any court in the land that the marriage was over. But until meeting Dante she had been reluctant to do anything about it, perhaps deep down she had been afraid of maybe having to face her ex-husband again. Stupid, she knew, but even now she still couldn't seem to throw off a niggling unease...

Dante was watching her with dark, pleading eyes; his proposal might have sounded casual, but she knew he was a hundred per cent sincere. 'Yes' was such a simple word, but suddenly Lexi shivered. A ghost walking over her grave; it couldn't be anything else—the temperature was a boiling ninety-five degrees. But somehow, with the mention of honeymoon and the thought of the irrevocable step she was about to take, she was no longer so sure.

'*Cara*, say something.'

'Yes, yes, that will be fine. November.' She said the words and smiled as Dante reached across the table and, catching her hand in his, gently squeezed her fingers, before planting a kiss on the back of her hand.

'Thank you, *cara*, I promise you won't ever regret marrying me.' Then his lips parted in a cheeky grin. 'Signor Monicelli will be delighted to stand with you; I took the liberty of asking him, on your behalf, last week.' And, letting go of her hand, he picked up his fork and continued eating.

Lexi shook her head, and smiled at his confidence, then followed suit, but her mind wasn't on her food, delicious though it was. The mention of Signor Monicelli had sent her thoughts spinning back to when she had arrived in Sorrento for the first time. She had stayed in London one night with her friend Cathy, after the painful betrayal by Jake. The following day Cathy had whisked her off to her parents' house in Surrey, and two days later Lexi had found herself travelling with Cathy's parents to Italy, where Cathy's father was taking up the post as British consul in Naples. Mr Clarke-Smythe had introduced her to Signor Monicelli, the owner of the Piccolo Paradiso and the Italian, once assured of her gift for languages and former brief stint in the Forest Manor hotel, had given her a job as a receptionist...

She had been lucky. Because of the haste of her first marriage her passport had not been changed from her maiden name of Miss Alexandra Laughton, consequently, with the exception of Signor Monicelli—she had mentioned it to him because it had seemed the right thing to do—and Dante, of course, no one else knew she had once been married.

Dante had been, and still was, a great friend of Signor Monicelli's son Marco, and that was how Lexi had got to know him. Up until last year Marco had been the hotel manager until a horrific car smash had left him paralysed from the waist down. Now he lived on the paradise island of Ischia with his parents and Lexi had been promoted to manage the hotel. But she knew Signor Monicelli was in the process of selling the hotel. Still, she thought musingly, even if the worst scenario occurred and the new owners did not want to employ her as manager, would it matter that much, now she was committed to marrying Dante?

She would regret losing her job, and she knew without any false pride that she was very good at what she did. But as there was some hope, if Signor Monicelli took his son to America, of Marco being taught to walk again, and he wanted to give Marco every chance, her own worries about unemployment were of no account.

Later, as dusk was falling, Lexi manoeuvred her little car back up the road to home, if not exactly ecstatic, she was feeling happily content at the future before her. Dante adored her. Admittedly, his kisses did not set her on fire, but they were loving and pleasurable, and she had no doubt when they finally married she would discover that his lovemaking was equally nice. Much as he teased her about going to bed with him, he was quite content to wait until they were married. Another big plus in his favour.

She shook her head as she got out of the car at the entrance to the hotel. What was she thinking about, adding up the plus signs like an accountant? And with a light step she ran up the stairs and into the foyer. It was a shame Dante had had to curtail their day out, but unfortunately the manager of his Amalfi shop had taken suddenly ill and Dante had to leave her to go and look after the shop himself.

Actually, she was relieved in a way; tonight she had a feeling she would not have been the best of company, as thoughts of the past flickered through her mind again. She stopped at the reception desk with a smile for Franco that did not quite reach her eyes and asked automatically, 'Any messages?'

Somehow all day she had been swinging between the past and present with alarming frequency, and she knew the cause; it was the same every year on the anniversary of her miscarriage, she thought ruefully, knowing she was being stupidly sentimental. Turning all her attention on Franco, she listened as he told her Signor Monicelli wanted her to call him urgently.

Picking up the telephone on Reception, she quickly dialled her boss's number. Five minutes later she replaced the receiver her lovely face wreathed in smiles. Apparently, the hotel sale had gone through, and the good news was that all the staff, herself included, were to remain in their jobs. She did not question why only minutes earlier she had accepted that she would leave work on her remarriage. She didn't dare admit even to herself the possibility that she loved her work more than Dante, but the lightness in her heart told its own story as she turned back to Franco, still grinning. 'Everything else OK?' she asked.' No more double-booking, I hope!' she teased with a mock frown.

Poor Franco, only the week before, had discovered a booking made by Anna, a junior, for a honeymoon couple registered to stay in a suite already occupied by a very important Arab guest. Luckily Lexi had been able to sort it out, but she had had to give her own, the manager's suite to the young couple, and spend the next few days sharing a room with Anna, the trainee receptionist.

'Not double-booked exactly.' Franco replied quite seriously.

'What? You haven't, not again!' Lexi's eyes narrowed keenly on his attractive face. When it came to business she was a hundred per cent efficient and she expected the same from her staff. Piccolo Paradiso was a favourite of a few seriously rich clients. People who appreciated the peace and quiet, the first-class service and absolute discretion of the management.

'No, no,' Franco responded, but Lexi noticed he avoided her eyes. 'But the gentleman was most insistent about seeing you...'

'I wouldn't take no for an answer,' a deep harsh voice echoed in her head.

Lexi swung around and the air left her lungs in a rush; she paled beneath her tan, her small hand reaching out to curl around the edge of the reception desk to give herself some support as her eyes widened to their fullest, extent in horror on the man before her. Of course, she should have known; it was the man in the black Bugatti. Jake . . . her husband.

'Why the surprise, Lexi? Surely you must have been expecting me,' he opined hardly, his dark blue eyes, as cold as the arctic wastes, sweeping her from head to toe with insulting sexual insolence. 'The curt note from your solicitor to mine informing me you were divorcing me was bound to elicit a response. That was your intention, was it not?'

She straightened her shoulders and let go of the desk. 'No, Mr Taylor.' Her chin tilted defensively as she held his hard gaze. 'In fact, I'm amazed you even know about the divorce.'

'My solicitor heard from yours yesterday, and immediately faxed me. What did you expect?' His smile was chilling. 'That'd I'd let you?' he drawled, and a *frisson* of alarm skidded down her spine.

'I never expected to see you again.' Her eyes dropped, slanting over his tall frame. If anything, he was even more arresting then she remembered. His handsome face was a little thinner, the lines bracketing his sensuous mouth slightly deeper, and his once night-black hair was now lightly sprinkled with grey, but it did nothing to detract from the potent, almost animal sexuality of the man. His broad shoulders and fine-honed frame were clad in hip-hugging jeans and a soft-knit shirt that only served to reinforce his lethal attraction.

A shiver of, not fear, but something more shaming made the fine hair on her skin stand erect. She felt nineteen again and stunned at the immensity of her reaction to this man. She hated him, but was horrified to realise he was still able to elicit an instant sexual response in her feminine body.

She was suddenly conscious of her skimpy blue jersey dress and bare legs, her long hair falling down her back in wild disarray. She knew she looked as though she had just walked off the beach and wished like hell she was attired in her uniform, a neat black suit and crisp white shirt. With a shaking hand she defensively tucked a few wild tendrils of hair behind her ear.

'Do I pass?'

His deep voice rasped along her overstretched nerves. She couldn't believe what a fool she had been! It had never occurred to her that Jake would respond to her solicitor's formal notification of the impending divorce in person. Her brows drew together in a puzzled frown. Why on earth would he want to? They had had no contact in almost five years. Surely Jake would be as happy as her at the ending of the marriage.

'If that frown is anything to go by, don't bother to answer—I probably wouldn't like your reply. Instead, let's find somewhere to talk.' He stepped towards her. Lexi tried to step back, his great height intimidating her, but was brought up hard against the reception desk.

'That will not be necessary,' Lexi managed in a taut voice. 'We have nothing to say to each other.' Her gaze once more met his and her violet eyes widened at the dark threat she saw in the deep blue depths of Jake's.

'You might find my presence abhorrent, Lexi, but I, I am not finished with you, not by a long way,' he told her in a hateful drawl. 'The next few weeks should be entertaining.'

'If you were thinking of staying here, Mr Taylor...the hotel is full.' She desperately tried to hang on to her business persona, but the shock to her system made her voice shake.

'So you say, but...'

'I am the manager, I know...' Her violet eyes sparkled with barely controlled anger, as some of her self-control returned. 'I think you should leave.' She gestured with her hand towards the entrance, and she bit her lip as Jake's strong hand caught her wrist in a painful grip.

'Let me go,' she hissed, her eyes stormy with pent-up anger as she tried to wrench her arm free.

'Nobody dismisses me with the wave of a hand, and certainly not a mercenary little bitch like you...' Jake snarled. His face hardened into an expression that made Lexi wish she hadn't tried so cavalierly to dismiss him as he continued. 'Now, if you wish to discuss our marriage in the foyer of the hotel, I really don't mind,' he informed her ruthlessly. 'I'm sure the rest of the guests will enjoy it.'

A chill shivered its way down the length of her spine as he dropped her wrist. With her other hand she rubbed where he had touched her, and what did he mean, mercenary? She didn't have a mercenary bone in her body, and she had never taken a penny from Jake since the day she left him.

'Is everything all right, Signorina Lexi?' Franco's voice intruded warily.

'Yes. Yes, fine,' Lexi confirmed swiftly as she glanced quickly around. Oh, God! The guests were on their way to dinner, and here she was looking like something the cat dragged in, arguing in the middle of Reception.

'Signorina Lexi... Odd, I could have sworn you were my wife,' Jake prompted with sardonic cynicism. 'Still, I suppose I should be grateful you appear to be working for a living. I fully expected you to have some wealthy lover looking after you.'

Lexi's head swung back to look at Jake, her mouth falling open in stunned amazement. 'Why, you...' Words failed her, which was probably just as well, she thought a moment later, remembering where she was.

'Or perhaps you're between keepers, hmm?'

Lexi registered the gasp of astonishment from Franco behind the desk. 'You are married to this man?' Franco exclaimed, and then broke out in a torrent of Italian, mostly about what Dante would say.

Lexi groaned inwardly and tried in a few words to calm her excitable assistant down. But finally she had no other course than to admit Jake was her husband.

'When you two have quite finished.' Jake's curt command stopped them both, his piercing gaze fixed on Franco. 'Perhaps you would arrange for my luggage to be taken to my wife's suite.'

For Lexi it was the last straw; she wanted to scream at Jake to shut up, but she knew she had to get him out of the reception before the whole damn place heard his revelation. 'Follow me,' she snarled between clenched teeth.

'I knew you would see it my way, Lexi, sensible girl,' he goaded mockingly.

She was too angry to take the lift, but preceded Jake up to the third floor and along to the far end of the corridor, her rage mounting at every step. She turned the key in the lock and opened the door. She didn't bother to look if Jake was behind her, but stormed across the room, flinging her bag on to a convenient sofa, and turned with her back to the window.

'Now, what the hell do you think you're playing at, Jake? How dare you come here and insinuate about my morals, or lack of them, in front of my staff and guests? Then to announce to the world we're married! You've got some damn nerve.' She was in a full-blooded fury, years of anger and frustration racing to the forefront of her mind.

'Is it so strange that I object to hearing my wife addressed as Mi-ss...?' Jake emphasised cynically.

'Dear God! You're mad. We have been separated for five years—five years, Jake. In fact, I can't understand why you didn't divorce me years ago, or why the hell you are here now, instead of cavorting around London with your faithful Lorraine,' she grated furiously.

'Then let me enlighten you, my sweet,' Jake drawled, a thread of steel in his voice. 'I have come to reclaim my wife.'

Her breath caught in her throat at his sheer arrogance. Her body trembling with fury, she cried, 'Don't be ridiculous.' Her voice shook with the force of her anger. 'You can't just walk into my life and say you're going to reclaim it.' She had hated this man for years; he had taken her girlish dream of love and family and forever and ground it in the dust beneath his feet. She was older now, a mature working woman, and no way would she put herself back in the subservient position of Jake's wife. 'I won't tolerate it.'

Jake, his dark eyes fixed on her flushed and furious face, slowly strolled across the room to stop only inches away from her. 'No more than I will tolerate some curt note from a solicitor telling me I am to be divorced.' The deadly intent in his softly voiced comment was more frightening than if he had shouted at her. 'You, Lexi, are my wife, and divorce is not an option, not now, not ever. Do I make myself clear?' he prompted silkily.

She had taken as much as she could stand; he was much too close, much too threateningly male. Without warning, her hand flew in a wild arc towards his mocking face, and she yelped with pain as he stopped her before she could make contact. His strong hand like a manacle around her wrist, in one deft movement he forced her hand down and behind her back, bringing her slap up against his hard body. In a second he had both her hands pinned by one of his much larger ones behind her back, and his dark head was swooping down.

Lexi tried to fight, but his arm was like an iron girder around her slender waist. She attempted to kick him, but was quickly trapped between his powerful thighs. Heat, totally unexpected, flooded through her body at their intimate entwining, and she could do nothing to prevent Jake using his free hand to grasp her chin and tilt her small face up to his.

'I will not tolerate violence, not even from you, Lexi.' Then his hard mouth crushed down on hers.

Fiercely she pressed her lips together, but the savagery of his kiss was not to be denied. His teeth nipped her bottom lip and her lips parted on a startled gasp of pain. His tongue plunged into her mouth, seeking out the moist dark corners with erotic expertise that took her breath away.

She vowed she would show no response—she hated him, had done for years. His hand slid from her chin to caress her throat and lower, the kiss gentled into an evocative, teasing caress and she felt something inside her leap to instant life as she threw her head back to avoid his kiss! No—to give him better access to the soft skin of her throat. His lips found the vulnerable hollow at the base of her neck, and her pulse-rate leapt alarmingly as her body responded with long-denied passion.

His free hand stroked down and edged inside the soft cotton neckline of her dress, to caress the soft, creamy mound of her breast—she was not wearing a bra—and, as his fingers stroked the burgeoning tips, bringing them to hard aching nubs of desire, she was helpless, drowning in a sea of passion she had thought lost to her forever. She felt the force of his masculine arousal, hard against her stomach, and a low moan escaped her.

'That's it, Lexi, let go.' His throaty voice quivered across the soft curve of her cheek, before his lips once more claimed hers. Fire coursed through her veins, lighting every nerve and sense, until she moved restlessly in an attempt to assuage the desperate hunger consuming her.

She was hardly aware her hands were now free, so lost in her abandoned descent into passion was she, nor that her dress had been slipped down her shoulders. She cried out as his mouth closed over her aching breast to tease the rigid tip with his teeth and tongue, and her own small hand grasped his muscular bicep as he bent her over his arm, his sensuous mouth suckling, grazing, teasing her into insensibility. Her other hand tangled in the thick silk hair of his head, urging him closer.

Then suddenly she was free. Her violet eyes, deep purple with passion, stared up into his darkly flushed face. 'Jake...?' she queried, still enslaved by his passionate assault.

Jake straightened, and with insultingly steady hands slipped her dress back up on to her shoulders. His dark eyes seared triumphantly down into hers. 'Later, Lexi; there's someone at the door. My luggage I expect.'

Only then did she hear the rat-tat-tat at the door. Her face burned with shame. God! What had she done? Jake had only had to touch her and she had burst into flames...

She was trembling, her legs would barely support her and, taking a few faltering steps, she collapsed on the sofa. She looked across the room as Jake opened the door to admit the young man with his luggage.

'Put it in the bedroom, please,' he commanded, and not a flicker of emotion disturbed the even tenor of his voice.

Lexi gazed in something like despair as the bellboy walked straight across the room and through into the bedroom, avoiding looking at her. She had employed the young man herself last year and it hurt to see him ignore her and to see the obvious embarrassment on his face. God, what had she done to deserve this? she wondered helplessly. And, resting her head in her hands, her elbows on her knees, it took every bit of will-power she possessed not to burst into tears. She could feel the moisture pricking at the back of her eyelids; she swallowed hard on the lump that formed in her throat and, slowly lifting her head, she ran her hands through the tumbled mass of her Titian hair, shoving it ruthlessly behind her ears.

She was a two-time loser, she thought bitterly. She hated Jake with a passion that had not dimmed in five long years... Yet her traitorous body still yearned for him. She cursed silently under her breath; how had she allowed the arrogant swine to walk in and walk all over her, yet again? Would she never learn?

Worse, her job was very important to her, but how was she going to be able to keep the respect of her staff after this? Even supposing she could get rid of Jake immediately, already the rumours must be rife. The manager ensconced in her suite with a husband nobody knew she had. It was a mess, a complete and utter disaster...

She felt the brush of a hand across her head, and she jumped in her seat.

'Take it easy, Lexi; we'll talk later. First I need to wash and change.'

She didn't answer, she couldn't; instead she watched with a kind of detached fascination as Jake strode across in front of her and into the bedroom. She stared at the door long after he had closed it behind him, heard the faint sound of running water, and her mind presented her with a memory of herself and Jake in the shower. She blinked furiously to dispel the image, and gazed around her.

This was her sanctuary: the pleasant lounge tastefully decorated in blue and gold, the ornate antique Italian-style furniture. The elegant desk, the two soft blue velvet sofas, a hotel suite, but also her home, with her own books on the shelves. She was happy here, and in less than an hour Jake had destroyed her peace, her contentment, her life. It was so unfair, all she wanted was to be free of the man.

Then it hit her: she had nothing to worry about, Jake's agreement was not necessary; in a few short weeks she could divorce him whether he liked it or not. Firmly, she took herself to task. She had been reacting, not acting, and it had to stop... She would hear Jake out, and then send him off with a flea in his ear. Maybe sexually he still had power over her. Who was she kidding? Never mind maybe, he did: her breasts were still tender from his touch; she ran the tip of her tongue over her swollen lips and the taste of him was still in her mouth. She was like a moth to his flame and always had been . . .

But she was twenty-five, a mature adult woman; surely she could resist him for the short time he would be here? Or perhaps the lovely Lorraine would appear on the scene and Lexi's troubles would be over. She sighed. Why hadn't Jake married Lorraine? When Lexi had settled in Italy and informed her solicitor of her address she had watched the post, expecting any day Jake's request for a divorce. When it had never arrived she'd worried, but as the months turned to years she had gradually put it out of her mind.

Suddenly it hit her! Jake was a ruthless businessman. He had married Lexi to get his hands on the manor and turn it into a paying venture, but Lorraine had no asset Jake coveted other than her body, and he wouldn't waste a marriage vow on that.

CHAPTER FOUR

'YOUR turn for the bathroom.'

Lexi jumped to her feet as Jake walked back into the room, and she had to stifle a gasp at his appearance. His black hair was still wet from the shower and brushed severely back from his broad forehead, giving his ruggedly attractive features a harder, more ruthless definition. He was dressed in a conventional black dinner-suit, the perfectly tailored jacket emphasising the width of his broad shoulders, the white silk shirt contrasting sharply with his sun-bronzed skin. Pleated trousers fitted snugly over his hips. He looked magnificently male yet somehow predatory as he casually strolled across the room and lowered his long length on to the sofa.

He glanced up at Lexi, his dark gaze sliding lazily over her. 'I've been travelling all night and half the day; I'm hungry, so be quick,' he commanded. 'And leave your hair loose; I like it that way.'

'Now wait a minute.' Lexi finally found her voice, he was not moving in on her and taking over her life, not again . . .'

'Really, Lexi, you never used to be so argumentative. Run along and get ready, unless of course you prefer we eat here.' His hand went to the tie at his neck. 'It might be more intimate, at that,' he opined mockingly.

Fuming, Lexi picked up her bag from the sofa and dashed to the safety of the bedroom. She flung her bag on the bed and stopped, her eyes widening in furious amazement. The devil had deliberately laid out a pair of black silk pyjamas on the bed—a blatant statement of intent. Well, she would show him, she vowed, marching across to the bathroom, pulling her dress over her head as she went. Jake might think he had won, but he had a rude awakening coming. She would have dinner with him, and if he refused to see sense about the divorce and go quietly, he could keep the damn suite and she would share with Anna again.

Naked, she stepped into the shower and turned on the tap, telling herself there was no way she was going to jeopardise her chance of a divorce. Another six weeks and Jake could do nothing to stop her, provided they stayed separated...

Standing under the soothing spray, she was tantalisingly aware of the lingering trace of Jake's cologne, the vital male scent of him still pervading the air from his recent occupancy of the bathroom. She was forced to admit it was far too big a risk being in the same room as the man. She shivered and, turning off the water, stepped out. It was only fifteen minutes ago that she had been putty in his hands. His lethal male charm still had the power to make her quake, and she couldn't afford to give in, not now. Not when she was so close to her goal.

Picking up a large, soft towel, she briskly dried herself, and walking into the bedroom opened a drawer and pulled out a flimsy cream lace bra and matching briefs. She slipped them on, and, crossing to the fitted wardrobes, extracted a pair of cream silk, softly pleated culottes with a matching sleeveless silk blouse. In seconds she was dressed, and, straightening the gold-trimmed collar that complemented the gold leather belt she cinched tightly around her small waist, she silently vowed that there was no way Jake was sharing her bed—not now, not ever, even if she ended up sleeping in the laundry cupboard! She hated him with a depth of feeling she had not believed herself capable of.

Briskly she brushed her hair and casually twisted it into a loose chignon on top of her head. The addition of a moisturiser to her face, a touch of dark mascara to her long lashes and the use of a soft pink lip-gloss to her full lips completed her toilet.

Finally she slipped her feet into high-heeled gold sandals, and, efficiently transferring a few basics from her bag on the bed to a small gold shoulder-bag, she straightened her shoulders and, taking a deep breath, re-entered the sitting-room.

The sofa was empty. She looked around; Jake was standing at the darkened window, his body in profile as he stared out into the night, seemingly unaware of her presence. For a moment she allowed her eyes to linger on him; was it tension she sensed in his huge frame? No, it couldn't be... His hard, chiselled features were curiously still, almost brooding. He turned, and his eyes locked with hers. His expression was impossible to define, and for some unknown reason Lexi felt menaced by the fraught quality of the silence between them, but she could not tear her gaze away.

Jake broke the contact; his dark eyes lowered, conducting a slow, sweeping survey of her feminine form before returning to her face, and she sensed a hint of disapproval, but why she had no idea. It was a designer outfit she had bought in the winter sale at an exclusive boutique on the isle of Capri.

'Very elegant, and expensive, no doubt.' Jake commented distastefully, his face hard with something like disgust as he moved towards her. 'But I told you to leave your hair loose.' And before she could object his strong hands had deftly unpinned her hair so it fell in a red cloud around her shoulders.

'Your days of telling me what to do are long gone,' she snapped, bitterly resentful, her hatred burning brighter as she remembered the months and years it had taken her simply to stop dreaming about the swine. She bit down hard on her lip. She would not let him taunt her into losing her temper; instead she deliberately swept her long hair back off her face. 'Don't you realise I have my position as manager to think of?' she informed him caustically.

'Not for much longer,' he declared arrogantly.

Lexi knew she should demand an explanation for his remark but he was standing within inches of her, and she could almost feel the warmth of his body; the sheer animal magnetism of the man had the power to stir her senses as no one else she had ever known. Shocked and greatly disturbed, she made no comment. Instead she headed for the door; retreat was the only option she was capable of pursuing.

The dining-room of the hotel was luxurious and intimate, and, as Lexi walked across the room with Jake at her side, his large hand firmly clasping her elbow, to the casual observer they looked like the perfect loving couple. The man tall and strikingly attractive and the woman small and exquisite, her eyes sparkling and her face flushed with pleasure. Only a very close observer would see that it was rage that put fire in her eyes and colour in her face.

By the time they were finally seated at Lexi's usual table she was so furious she wanted to hit Jake. As she had spoken to various guests, Jake had delighted in introducing himself as her husband, completely ignoring her acute embarrassment.

'What the hell do you think you're playing at?' she hissed as she carefully folded her napkin on her lap. Her eyes flashed angrily across to her companion. 'I suppose you think that was a huge joke telling Miss Davenport you're my husband. Only last week she met my boyfriend; what on earth is she going to think? And she's one of our best customers.'

Jake's mouth curved derisively. 'Hardly my fault, Lexi, my dear; you should have had more sense than to acquire a boyfriend when you still have a husband.'

She flung up her head, fury leaping in her eyes. 'I don't have a husband, I haven't...'

'Had me in years. I know, but tonight I intend to correct that,' he drawled smoothly, his glance sweeping down to the deep V of her shirt, and lingering on her exposed creamy cleavage with lascivious intent.

'That was not what I meant and you know it, you...you...pervert,' she shot back, the colour in her face almost matching her hair.

His dark features hardened immeasurably 'I will not tolerate opposition, Lexi. I have let you run free far too long, but not any more.' His eyes held hers with un-wavering scrutiny. 'Fight me and I will fight back, and I can assure you I always win.'

Her eyes warred angrily with his. This was one fight Lexi had to win, to keep her self-respect, her pride. Her life. How would she have answered? She never knew, as the waiter appeared at the table.

'Would madam and sir like to order now?' The pointed use of madam only fuelled Lexi's anger.

'A pasta Genovese, followed by steak, medium, for me, and shall I order for you, Lexi darling? I know your taste so well.' Jake's question was a silken-voiced taunt that made her see red.

'I'm not hungry,' she snapped at the poor waiter. 'No starter, and anything. Veal Marsala, whatever.'

Jake sat back in his chair, his dark eyes resting on her flushed face. 'Is that any way for the manager to treat staff? The man was only doing his job.'

'I never lose my temper with staff.' Lexi managed to keep her voice low. 'It's only you, and your presence here, that makes me lose my temper.'

'Funny, when we first met you never argued with me. In the beginning I used to wonder when the famous red-headed temper would show itself, until I married you and discovered you saved all your fire and passion for making love.'

Suddenly, kaleidoscopic images of herself and Jake in bed together filled her mind with erotic clarity. She briefly closed her eyes to dispel the images, and when she opened them again, Jake was slowly assessing every one of her features, from her red face to the small hand that lay on the table, the fingers clenched in outrage, and, when he returned his gaze to hers, she had to fight to keep herself from trembling. Luckily the wine waiter intervened and the next few moments Jake spent choosing the wine, a rather good Barola, while Lexi fought to regain some self-control, which unfortunately deserted her immediately Jake opened his mouth again.

'Your present lover—Dante, isn't it?' He smiled but the smile never reached his eyes, as the intensity of his gaze nailed her to the spot. 'It seems he does not take after his namesake. Dante's *Inferno*. It is obvious he lights no fire in you, Lexi; if he did, you wouldn't have the passion to cross swords with me, or melt in my arms as you did earlier in the bedroom.'

'Will you shut up...? People will hear...' Lexi cast a frantic glance at the tables around them. Thank God no one seemed to have overheard. 'This is a very exclusive hotel, and I am responsible for it.' She took refuge in her professional role, mainly because she had a nasty feeling there might have been some truth in Jake's jeering remark and she did not want to examine her own emotions too closely.

Jake slanted her a sardonic glance. 'But of course you're quite right. I would hate the hotel to lose any custom because the manager went crazy in the dining-room. Terrible for business, especially now.'

Sarcastic pig! She muttered under her breath, but, fighting down the urge to retaliate, Lexi forced herself to remain calm. She heaved a sigh of relief when the wine waiter returned with the requested bottle and after allowing Jake to taste it filled both their wine-glasses.

Jake raised his glass to her. 'Well, isn't this nice? Quite like old times, Lexi. You and I sharing an expensive, intimate meal together.' And, lifting the glass to his firm mouth, he swallowed the rich red liquid. But the mocking light in his dark eyes belied his innocent comment.

For a moment Lexi had felt a brief regret for the past. When they were first married, and lived in London, they had used to eat out a lot, sampling the meals on offer in some of the best restaurants in the capital. She had been so in love, filled with such hope for the future... Hastily, she picked up her glass and took a gulp of the wine in an attempt to steady her nerves and dismiss the painful memories. She ignored Jake as another waiter placed a plate of pasta in front of him. That will shut him up, she thought thankfully. But what did he mean, 'especially now'? She banished the irritating thought, and began to get her mind in gear. How did Jake know about Dante? She hadn't told her solicitor why she wanted the divorce. In fact, she had given her solicitor strict instructions not to tell anyone, especially not Jake, where she was living.

'How did you know where to find me?' The question slipped out involuntarily. Her mind was spinning like a windmill and it was all Jake's fault. She cast him a baleful glance across the table. His dark head was bent and there was no doubt he was enjoying his food; he made love with the same wholehearted enjoyment as he relished fine food, enjoying every taste and... Annoyed, she clamped down on the wayward thought.

'I asked...' she began.

'I heard you.' His dark head lifted, his blue eyes clashed with hers. 'I have known for years where you were.'

'But how?' she asked, taken back by his revelation.

'We have a mutual acquaintance. Mr Carl Bradshaw.'

Her brow furrowed in a frown as she searched her memory; the name rang a bell.

'He was a regular customer at this hotel, before he married. Apparently he was staying here the spring after you arrived. By sheer coincidence I had business dealings with the man. We were sharing lunch when he showed me a photograph of you taken by the swimming-pool here. He was bemoaning the fact he had met a gorgeous girl who had actually said no to him. I recognised you immediately, but I didn't bother telling him you were my runaway wife,' he offered cynically. 'You slipped up there, Lexi; Carl Bradshaw is one of the wealthiest men in Europe.'

Lexi remembered the man, and he had asked her out, but at the time she had been still raw and bleeding from Jake's betrayal. But what did Jake mean, she had slipped up? She heard the words and assimilated them but it made no sense. All this time Jake had known where to find her and yet only now had he bothered. And what did he mean, she had run away? He had freely admitted he wanted out of the marriage, she had heard him with her own ears declare to his mistress, Lorraine, his intention of breaking their marriage vows. Her nerves stretched to breaking point, she lowered her head to escape his gimlet-like gaze, and, picking up her glass, took a sip of the soothing wine.

Carefully, she placed the glass back down on the table, and, regaining her self-control, she glanced up. 'So why turn up now?' she demanded coldly.

For a long moment he just looked at her. A muscle tautened along the edge of his jaw, and his eyes darkened with icy bleakness. 'I do not appreciate my wife acquiring a permanent boyfriend and suing me for divorce. I decided to put a stop to it,' he declared arrogantly.

'Some hope; we're engaged.'

'Not any more, you're not.' His dark eyes narrowed on her mutinous face. 'Tell me, Lexi, why do you think your so-called fiancé was called away this evening?' he questioned with thinly veiled mockery.

'You—you arranged it.' She looked at him in horrified amazement. 'But how? In fact, how did you know about Dante?'

'I had you investigated, months ago.'

Months ago, but he couldn't have known then that she was suing for divorce, she hadn't known herself.

'As for your friend, as you know better than most——' contempt lurked in his eyes '—people will do anything for the right price. Hence your friend's manager took conveniently ill, and I did not have to waste time waiting around for you.'

'Bu...bu...but...' As she spluttered with rage, Lexi's violet eyes flashed fire. 'How dare you?' she finally cried, rather inanely.

'I dare anything to get what I want, Lexi, and make no mistake, I want you.' His steely gaze seemed to sear through to her soul. 'And now I can afford you.'

'Afford me...' she burst out. Of all the hypocritical swine, he took the biscuit. It wasn't enough that he had married her in the first place simply to take over her family home; he had the audacity to insinuate that she was mercenary. She picked up her knife, longing to stick it in his hateful, mocking face.

His dark head angled towards her. 'Don't even think it, Lexi,' he hissed with sibilant softness. 'And I suggest, unless you want the whole of the restaurant to know your business, that you shut up and eat up.'

How did he walk into her mind like that? Lexi thought, but before she could form a reply the waiter placed the main course in front of her. She had been so caught up in her own emotional turmoil that she had not noticed the man's arrival...

Oh, what was the use? she thought wretchedly, her shoulders slumping dejectedly as she picked up her fork and began to push the food around her plate. Jake was a master at getting his own way. If she had any sense at all, it would pay her to spend the rest of the meal ignoring the man and marshalling her thoughts into some kind of order.

Lexi picked at the superb food; it could have been ashes for all she cared. She drank the wine and that helped to restore her confidence a little, but it was false courage and she knew it. She glanced across at Jake, who was eating his steak with every sign of enjoyment. He caught her look and his firm mouth curved in the briefest of smiles.

'The food is exquisite; I must compliment the chef,' he offered smoothly.

'Do that,' Lexi grunted, and looking at her watch she noted it was almost ten. The sooner she could get the confrontation with Jake over and done with, the quicker she could get him out of her life.

'Shall we adjourn to the lounge for coffee?' his deep voice queried, meticulously polite.

Not deigning to look at him Lexi shoved back her chair and stood up, determination in every line of her small frame. 'No, we can have it in my suite. We've spent long enough this evening avoiding the real issue. Shall we go?' And, not waiting for his response, she picked up her bag and walked through the dining-room, a stiff smile plastered on her face for the benefit of the few guests who bade her goodnight, and headed for the lift.

'Right, say what you have to say and leave,' Lexi demanded, standing rigidly in the middle of the room. Nervously she rubbed her damp palms over her hips. She was no way as in control as she sounded, but Jake couldn't possibly know that, she reassured herself. He was standing with his back to the door, his dark eyes slow and analytical as he swept her stiff body and back to her face.

'Sit down, Lexi.'

'That won't be necessary; I don't intend you will be here that long. I am a working girl; I have a busy day tomorrow, and I want to get to bed.'

'By all means, Lexi; we can talk in bed if that's what you prefer.'

He sounded amused, damn him. 'In your dreams, buster,' she burst out, her temper bubbling over. 'You have no right to come barging back into my life, telling everyone you're my husband, completely destroying my credibility with my staff. Just where the hell do you think you get off? I have had just about as much of you as I can stand, and if you don't leave in the next minute I will call the porter to throw you out. In fact, I can't understand why I didn't do it in the first place.'

In two strides Jake was beside her, his large hands closed over her slender shoulders, his fingers biting into the soft flesh. 'Enough, Lexi, screaming like a fishwife will get us nowhere.' He was right and, taking a deep breath, she fought down the *frisson* of awareness his touch aroused, and stepped back. He let her go...

'Have you finished shouting?' Jake asked quietly, subjecting her to a slow and intent appraisal that left her feeling wanting.

She had gone over the top a bit, and raising a hand to her brow she smoothed back the tangled strands of her long hair, and swallowed on her anger. 'Yes,' she said curtly. She had been finished with Jake long ago and yelling at the man wasn't going to solve anything. 'Please tell me what you came for, and go.'

'Sit down, Lexi.'

She subsided into the nearest chair and watched warily as Jake sat down on the sofa, his long legs stretched out in front of him in negligent ease.

'Now, isn't this more civilised, darling?' he drawled mockingly, while never taking his dark gaze from her flushed face.

'Get on with it, Jake.' She was in no mood for polite chit-chat.

'It's perfectly simple, Lexi, I told you earlier. I want you back as my wife, reinstated in my bed.'

It took a tremendous strength of will to retain a degree of civility, but somehow she managed it. 'Is that all?' she quipped lightly while her mind spun on oiled wheels. He was up to something, but what? He had said earlier that he wanted her back, and now he had reiterated the request, yet she knew it wasn't true. He didn't love her, never had, and why the thought should bring a flash of pain, she did not question. So what other reason could he possibly have...?

'I get it!' Lexi exclaimed. Of course, why hadn't she thought of it before? She sat back in the chair, a sigh of relief escaping her. It was so obvious; in a flash of blinding clarity she saw it all. Jake was a very wealthy man, and she knew to her cost that he would do anything for money. Divorce must have terrified him, because according to the law his wife could take half of his money half his business. No wonder the swine came hot-foot to Italy.

'Good, I am pleased. Then let's get to bed, it's been a long day,' Jake drawled facetiously.

'No, I understand, Jake.' She bent forward, her elbows on her knees, her serious gaze fixed on his face. 'You have nothing to worry about; I've instructed my lawyer. I don't want any alimony, not a penny. Your business, your investments, everything is safe. I don't want it. I'll sign a contract now, tonight, if you like.' And for the first time since meeting Jake again his lips parted in a genuine smile, even if it was a little self-satisfied.

There was no returning smile on Jake's handsome face. Instead his gaze became hooded and he rose to his feet to tower over her. 'Nice try, Lexi, but it won't work.'

'But——' she flashed him a puzzled look '—surely...' Perhaps he hadn't understood.

'You took me for a fool once, but never again. 'He reached down his strong hands, and grasping her upper arms, he hauled her to her feet, and, tilting her head back with one large hand, his chillingly bleak eyes locked on hers, trapping her in his gaze. 'You would no more give up a fortune than pigs would fly, and as for signing it away, forget it.'

'Why, you arrogant . . .' Before she could complete the sentence his dark head bent, his mouth covering hers in a harsh, bruising kiss. She twisted her head in a frantic effort to get away, her hand clawed at his shoulder while she kicked out at him with her feet, but with insulting ease Jake ground his mouth down on hers, the relentless pressure forcing her lips apart.

There was nothing she could do to prevent his plundering invasion, and to her horror she felt the betraying curl of desire ignite in her stomach. In a desperate effort to get him to desist she lifted her hand to his face and scratched the hard jawline.

Jake jerked his head back, and his dark eyes flared with inimical rage. 'You shouldn't have done that, Lexi,' he said with icy menace. He shifted his weight, trapping her helplessly against him; she tried to strike out at him, but with consummate ease he trapped both her hands in one of his between their two bodies.

Lexi's eyes widened to their fullest extent as she recognised the intention in Jake's black gaze. 'No, Jake.' She was powerless, held hard against him; she could feel the heat of his body through the fine fabric of her clothes, and to her horror she could feel his masculine arousal. Then she had no more chance to think, as his mouth once more took hers in a kiss that went on and on, becoming a ravaging, passionate possession that violated all her senses but paradoxically set her body on fire. She wanted to cry, 'Stop!' in shame and disgust, but instead her body softened, moving of its own volition to accommodate Jake's hard length.

She trembled uncontrollably as she felt his strong hand slide insolently over her shoulder and down into the open neck of her shirt. With a savage wrench, her blouse was open to her waist and his hand cupped the fullness of her breast. In seconds the bra was pushed from her breasts and his long fingers dragged tantalisingly over one rigid nipple; catching the aching peak, he nipped it between his finger and thumb as his mouth slid down to her throat, closing over the madly beating pulse in a wild lover's bite that took her breath away. She whimpered, a fierce pleasure, almost pain, burning through every nerve in her body, her stomach clenched in heated excitement. She was lost, a fierce primeval need sending the blood surging through her veins like molten fire.

Incredibly, it was over. Jake, with a muffled curse, shoved her away from him, and she fell in a crumpled heap on to the sofa behind her. For a moment she did not know what had happened; one second they had been clawing at each other in desperate sexual need and now she was collapsed on the sofa, his tall dark form towering over her. Lexi did not dare look at him. The traitorous response of her body filled her with bitter humiliation. She hated him, even as she still ached for his touch. But even worse was the knowledge that Jake must know her body had betrayed her.

'Cover yourself, woman,' Jake snarled contemptuously. 'You disgust me, and, God knows, I disgust myself.'

His words killed all trace of desire in her trembling body in an instant. An icy chill shivered along her skin and, struggling, she adjusted her tattered clothes. So, she disgusted him . . . Why did the words hurt? she wondered bleakly.

'I won't take you tonight.' Her head shot up at his words; he was standing about a foot away, his dark eyes glittering with an unholy light, his face flushed with the force of his rage, and the marks of her nails carved his jaw. Her gaze dropped to his strong hands curled into fists at his thighs, as if it was the only way he could stop himself lashing out at her.

'Chance would be a fine thing.' She tried to sneer. He hated her... it was there in every taut line of his large body, in the black depths of his eyes, and the cruel twist of his hard mouth. She could almost taste the hatred, an evil aura in the air.

'Chance has nothing to do with it. The way I feel right now it would be more an assault than making love.' The harsh, guttural comment froze her blood. 'That's what you drive me to, you little witch.'

Lexi gasped, and clenched her hands together at her breast in a futile gesture of self defence. Jake's glance dropped to her hands, and his mouth twisted in a bitter cynical curve.

'Don't worry, Lexi, you have nothing to fear. I will not sully the anniversary of our son's death by taking you in anger.'

'You remembered...' she whispered, stunned to realise that Jake had actually known this was the anniversary of her miscarriage, and, even more surprisingly, he had known the lost child was a boy. Her gaze flew to his dark, forbidding face, and she realised he had controlled his earlier rage.

Hooded lids dropped over his deep blue eyes, masking his expression as, with a negligent shrug of his broad shoulders, he said 'Of course, that's the main reason I'm here.'

Lexi didn't understand any of this. She supposed she should be thankful he was not going to share her bed. 'But...' she began, only to have the question stop in her throat as Jake went on.

'I want the child you owe me, but I also intend to make sure it's mine.'

He could not have hurt her more if he had tried. Once she would have given anything to have his child, but now... 'No... never...' She murmured the words more to herself than to him. She found it incredible that he could be so arrogant, so lacking in any moral conscience.

'Yes, my dear Lexi, though in the present circumstances I am going to have to wait a few weeks to be assured of the parenthood,' he said cynically 'I have no intention of being stuck with your boyfriend's offspring...'

'Why, you...' Lexi leapt to her feet as the meaning of his words hit her. 'I...'

'Not again, Lexi.' His arms swept around her and held her hard against him. 'Tomorrow you are coming with me, and I intend to watch you every minute of every day until the time is right, and then, my dear Lexi, you and I will resume our marriage fully. Understood?'

'You can't make me.' Though once more held firmly in his arms, she had a horrible feeling he probably could.

'If I let you go, will you endeavour to behave like a lady for a change and listen?' He smiled mockingly down into her once again flushed and furious face.

'Yes,' she got out between clenched teeth: she would do anything to escape his all too familiar embrace.

'Good.' And, lifting her off her feet, he deposited her once more on the sofa and sat down beside her, his hard thigh pressing lightly against her slender limbs. She eased along the sofa putting a little space between them. He shot her a cynically amused glance and then, leaning back in the seat, he steepled his long fingers in front of him, for all the world as if he was about to give a lecture.

'It is really quite simple, dear Lexi. I have bought this hotel. You are now employed by me.'

She couldn't believe it. 'You own... Then I'll resign...'

Ignoring her comment, he continued in a voice devoid of all emotion, 'Unless you do as I say, I will cancel the sale, and Signor Monicelli will not get the money, and his son will not recover.'

Her head spun as the implications of his words sank in. She flashed him an angry glance, hating him in that second more than she had in all the years they had been apart. 'There are other people in the world who might buy the hotel,' she shot back sarcastically. 'You are not the only businessman on the planet, even if you like to think you are,' she lashed out in fear. She did not like where the conversation was going.

'True,' he agreed silkily, his gaze never wavering from her taut, rebellious features. 'But aren't you forgetting an important factor?' he prompted smoothly, but the underlying steel in his tone was unmistakable. 'Time is of the essence for young Marco. This place has made only a modest profit in the last couple of years and I have the power to make it known that it is not a viable proposition,' he elaborated cynically. 'If young Marco's trip to America is delayed or cancelled, who knows?' He turned his hands palms up in a negligent gesture. 'It will be a great shame if he is condemned to a wheelchair all his life, simply because the money is not available for his treatment.'

Lexi stared in horror at his hard, chiselled features. Not a flicker of compassion lightened his indigo eyes. No! her mind screamed silently, she couldn't do it, tie herself to this man once again when she knew there was only hatred between them. 'Why—why me?' she asked dazedly. It didn't make any kind of sense...

One eyebrow arched sardonically. 'You're my wife. I'm a very wealthy man, I need an heir and I don't believe in divorce. Nor do I appreciate hearing my wife is thinking of marrying another man.'

He might as well have added *so there*, Lexi thought in stunned amazement. Obviously it must have been a blow to his pride to discover she had a boyfriend. How typically chauvinistic. It was all right for Jake to have an affair with his PA but the slightest rumour that his estranged wife might do the same and he was hot-foot to Italy to put a stop to it. Talk about double standards! But why was she so surprised? she asked herself sadly. This was the same man who had broken his marriage vow to her and then expected her to toast him and his girlfriend in champagne. The so-called civilised sophisticates, but Lexi had never been one of them.

With a jerky movement she staggered to her feet and walked across the room to gaze sightlessly out into the dark night. How could she be responsible for Signor Monicelli's losing the sale? For young Marco's perhaps being tied to a wheelchair for life? She spun around.

Jake had followed her and was standing a step away. She looked up at him, and it was a stranger's face she saw. 'Would you really condemn a man...?'

'Believe it.' Jake brutally cut her off, and she did... It was there in his mocking smile and the ruthless glint in his eyes. 'Technically, Lexi, it is only you who can condemn the man to his chair, not I,' he said callously, adding, 'Yes, or no, Lexi?'

It wasn't fair, she raged inwardly, Jake must know damn fine there was no way she could let the Monicellis down; they had virtually saved her sanity five years ago, and she owed them. Why now, she fumed, just when she had got her life in order? Dante... Dante; she had today promised to marry him.

'Dante... What can I tell him?' she cried in dismay, unconsciously giving her answer.

She did not see the flash of triumph in Jake's eyes before his expression hardened fractionally. 'You can ring him before we leave in the morning, but I will not allow you to see him,' he warned icily.

'Leave? I can't leave, I have my job...'

'Not any more.' And striding across the room he picked up the telephone receiver and dialled a number. 'Lorraine, get over to the Piccolo Paradiso first thing in the morning. I want you to take charge until a permanent manager can be found. OK... Goodnight.' Jake replaced the receiver and turned, a smile of triumph curving his hard mouth. 'Your replacement arrives in the morning.'

Lexi stood as though turned to stone at the mention of the other woman's name, her violet eyes blank as her thoughts turned inwards; Jake had it all arranged, must have been planning it for weeks. The fact she had started divorce proceedings had little or nothing to do with it.

'The divorce didn't matter?' she said to herself.

'No, not really. I had every intention of reclaiming you. The fax from my lawyer simply made me speed up the proceedings.'

'Lorraine.' She almost choked on the name. 'Why didn't you divorce me and marry her years ago?' she demanded. After all, it was what he had intended—she had heard them discussing it. She raised angry eyes to Jake's. 'She's still with you. Let her give you the heir you say you want,' she prompted sarcastically.

'Lorraine is much more valuable to my business than she could ever be as a wife and mother,' he offered casually.

'And that's it?' Lexi stared into his harsh face, unable to believe what she was hearing. 'You expect me to crawl back into your bed and provide you with a child.' She could not keep the shock and horror out of her voice. 'And at the same time, your mistress——'

'Why so surprised?' Jake cut in cynically. 'You've lived in Italy for years, you were planning on marrying an Italian. It's quite common in this part of the world for the wife and mother to be revered, while the mistress provides the fun.'

He meant it, he actually meant what he said. 'There is no way on this earth I will put up with an unfaithful husband. You should know that better than most, Jake,' she said scathingly. Hadn't she left him because of his infidelity?

'Should I?' he queried with a puzzled frown.

Lexi answered with a snort of disgust. Who was he kidding, pretending innocence? Certainly not her...

'Well, I suppose I can live with that. No Lorraine in my bed, and no Dante anywhere near you.' He smiled, a bleak twist of his hard mouth. 'Agreed.' And he held out his hand. 'Shake on it.'

Hardly knowing what she was doing, she put her hand in his. Lorraine, his mistress, or ex if Jake was to be believed, was near by, ready to take her job, the same way as she had taken Lexi's husband years ago. It was so evil her mind could not absorb it. He didn't even like her, and yet...

'You called me mercenary before, Jake; surely you don't want a gold-digger as the mother of your child?' she scorned in a last-ditch attempt to save herself.

'Let me worry about that, Lexi, you look tired. Get to bed, I have one or two more calls to make.' Jake's voice sounded almost gentle, but it could not mask the ruthless satisfaction she saw in his eyes.

'Yes, I'll go to bed,' Lexi agreed coldly. 'But first I want you to know I think you are utterly despicable, a man without conscience or morals, completely evil. I hate you and always will.' And the very softness of her tone was more convincing than any angry outburst could ever be.

CHAPTER FIVE

HEAD high, and stiff-backed Lexi marched into the bedroom. She would not give him the satisfaction of knowing he had frightened her into running away again. Anyway, hadn't he said himself that to touch her tonight would disgust him, she reassured herself as she undressed for bed. Hours later she plumped the pillow for the umpteenth time and, emotionally and mentally exhausted from trying to think of a way out of the disastrous situation she was in, she finally fell asleep, refusing to listen to the devilish imp inside her that traitorously wished Jake had joined her.

Lexi half opened her eyes, a distant ringing echoing in her head. Oh, God, the alarm—was it seven already? she thought sleepily and, automatically stretching out her hand, she silenced the offending clock on the bedside table. She groaned and suddenly froze, aware of a hard weight around her waist and the pressure of strong fingers curved around the underside of her breast. The full horror of the previous evening swamped her sleep-hazed mind. Jake was back and, worse, in her bed . . .

Slowly, she turned her head; Jake was lying flat on his stomach, one long arm flung across her waist, the other dangling over the side of the bed. She couldn't see his face, only the back of his head, the dark hair rumpled, and his heavy breathing loud on the still air. Tense, she held her breath, the warmth of his fingers through the fabric of her nightshirt arousing an achingly familiar response. She bit her lip, fighting down the swift stab of desire, and, making sure he was sound asleep, with the utmost caution she carefully slid out from under his arm, her feet finding the floor. She stopped as he grunted and turned over on to his back. It was OK, his eyes were still closed, and she was standing on his pyjamas!

She stood up, pulling her plain cotton nightshirt down over her thighs, and glanced down at the sleeping man. Completely relaxed, he looked years younger, his hair fell casually over his broad forehead, his firm mouth gentle in sleep. She had to restrain the urge to reach out and smooth his hair from his brow. His muscular chest with its dark covering of body hair rose and fell in an even rhythm, the single cotton cover was wrapped around his thighs, barely covering the core of his masculinity. His long arms and legs were spreadeagled across the bed; he looked devastatingly male, open and somehow vulnerable, waiting to be touched.

God! What was she thinking of? She shook her head in self-disgust and stealthily moved across the room, her nose wrinkled in irritation; there was a strong smell of alcohol in the air. She cast one last glance at the sleeping man before slipping into the bathroom. Surely Jake hadn't turned into a drinker! That was all she needed, a drunken husband.

Ten minutes later, bathed and dressed in her usual uniform of dark skirt and crisp white blouse, she cast one last glance at the still sleeping figure, her lips quirked in the semblance of a smile; he was going to have a hell of a hangover when he finally surfaced. Serve the swine right, she told herself, as she strode into the living-room. An empty whisky bottle and glass on an occasional table beside the sofa caught her gaze. Jake had certainly made a night of it, and she couldn't help wondering why.

She had stormed off to bed last night, knowing Jake had won but refusing to give up entirely. She had lain for hours unable to sleep, trying to find an escape, until finally she had virtually passed out, still wondering and fearing what the outcome of the evening's events would be. One option she had never considered was Jake getting plastered! It was hardly flattering to her; he was a powerful, dynamic male, and the years had not affected his masculine virility one bit. There was something about him, the way he moved, an earthy maleness that attracted the female of the species like bees around a honeypot. She doubted if any woman had ever left his bed unsatisfied, until now...

Dear God! She was doing it again, fantasising about the man. Annoyed with herself, she caught her rambling thoughts before they sank into eroticism. She was trapped and supposed to be finding a way out of the mess, not dreaming about the man.

Closing the door of the suite quietly behind her she slung her shoulder bag over her arm and headed for the lift. Moments later, she walked into the hotel reception and stopped, her eyes widening at the sight that met her eyes. Franco was standing, his mouth hanging open like a goldfish, while a tall, elegant woman was telling him in a cold, clipped voice exactly what to do. It was Lorraine...

'Excuse me,' Lexi said firmly, striding across to the desk. 'Have we some problem here?'

Lorraine spun around to face her. The older woman was as stunning as ever, perhaps a few more lines around her perfectly made-up eyes, and a hint of more hardness in the glossy mouth, but the smart cream suit she wore screamed designer original, as did the matching hide bag and shoes.

'Not any more, Lexi,' Lorraine stated flatly, her dark eyes glittering oddly. 'As of now, I am the manager by order of the new owner, as you know. Now, where is Jake? I need to speak with him.'

'And hello to you too, Lorraine,' Lexi murmured sarcastically. 'Still as super-efficient as ever, I see.' It hurt her to see her husband's mistress; she hated herself for the weakness, and tried to hide it behind a cool control she was far from feeling.

'If this man is anything to go by you could do with some efficiency around here. I have been trying for the past ten minutes to discover which room is Jake's.'

It gave Lexi great satisfaction to say, 'Franco probably didn't realise Jake is sharing my suite; I left him asleep, he's worn out, poor man.' She deliberately dropped her tone suggestively. 'But if you insist on disturbing him...' And she held out the key. Lorraine snatched it from her hand and stalked off to the stairs without a word.

'Is it true, Lexi, you're leaving?' Franco burst into impassioned speech; it took Lexi five minutes to calm him down and her explanation was inept, to say the least. Finally, fed up with the whole affair, she did what she should have done the night before. She walked out of the hotel and to her car, started the motor and drove off. She wasn't running away, she told herself, but she needed time, time to think, time to plan, and she owed it to Dante to see him and tell him what had happened.

She drove down into Sorrento looking in her rear-view mirror every few seconds, afraid of being followed, although her rational mind told her it was highly unlikely. Jake, even if he was awake, was probably in no fit state to drive, and anyway Lorraine was with him... Jake had agreed last night to complete fidelity when or if they resumed their marriage, but technically they had not yet consummated their reunion. Did that mean Lorraine even now was occupying the space Lexi had so recently vacated. In bed with Jake...

Lexi brought the car to a screaming halt outside a small café that was open early in the morning. Dante's apartment was two blocks away. She sat down at the bar counter and ordered a cappuccino. She drank the first cup in seconds, grateful for the reviving brew, and ordered another, along with a handful of loose change.

Feeling once more in control, she picked up the counter-top telephone and dialled Signor Monicelli's number. She was not beaten yet, she swore silently. She needed to know for herself if Jake's story was correct. Five minutes later she had her answer; by a bit of judicious questioning, Signor Monicelli had confirmed her worst fear: there was no way he could or would want to delay the hotel sale. He was expecting the cheque to be paid into his bank that morning and he was leaving with Marco tomorrow for America.

'That's great...' Lexi heard herself murmur, her heart in her feet.

'*Si, si.* I'm praying nothing goes wrong, and I am depending on you, Lexi, to work as well for the new owner as you have done for me. It would be disastrous if he takes up his option of pulling out within twelve months, and I don't get the final payment.'

'Final payment?' Lexi queried.

'Yes, the finance is arranged in three instalments; I get the final one in eighteen months' time. So remember, be nice to the man.'

At the mention of eighteen months, Lexi's half-formed plan to disappear as soon as she got the opportunity bit the dust.

Lexi dropped the phone back in its cradle, his last comment echoing in her head. 'Let me know when you and Dante are to marry and I will return for the ceremony.' What a joke! But it solved one puzzle. Signor Monicelli had not betrayed her. He obviously did not know Jake was her wayward husband.

Reluctantly she picked up the receiver once again and dialled Dante's number. He had already left for work. She glanced at her wrist. Damn! She had forgotten her watch. She looked up at the clock behind the counter and was surprised to see it was nine. She finished her second cup of coffee and rang Dante's shop. She did not want to call round as that would be the first place Jake would look, she was sure. When she replaced the receiver for the last time, she had to brush the moisture from her eyes. It was so unfair—Dante was a good, kind man and he didn't deserve what she was going to do to him.

She walked out of the bar, her footsteps slow and weary. It was a hot, clear morning, the sun brilliant in a clear, blue sky and the temperature was already in the eighties. Slowly, she walked across to her car and, getting in, sat behind the wheel. She was meeting Dante at nine-thirty and she needed to work out what she would say to him.

Lexi closed her eyes, her head falling forward to rest on her arms crossed over the steering-wheel. She had nowhere to run to. Her life and everything she owned was back at the hotel. A tear escaped to roll down her soft cheek. She thought of Marco and his father; she couldn't possibly hurt them. Jake had done his work well, she was trapped and at his mercy. But the man she had seen last night didn't know the meaning of the word 'mercy'. She had seen it in his face, in his cold-blooded determination to have his own way. He was a ruthless bastard who would stop at nothing to get what he wanted.

She remembered the week before her marriage. She had assumed, because Jake had asked her to marry him and offered to pay her father's debt, that they would naturally keep Forest Manor, and he had quite coolly told her that nothing had changed in that respect, the house would still be converted to a hotel, though he promised her he would convert part of the building into an apartment for their own use. So she would not really be losing her home. With hindsight, she realised she should have known then that Jake was the type of man who never wavered in his resolve to get what he wanted. Instead it had taken her almost a year and the loss of her baby to discover just what a conniving swine he was.

She lifted her head, a deep sigh escaping her. She had no idea what she was going to tell Dante; she only knew she could not tell him the truth. He was the type of man who would insist on standing by her and fighting for what was right. But Jake was a vicious enemy and deep down she knew Dante would be no match for him. Jake would gobble him up and spit him out if Dante attempted to thwart his plan.

Lexi walked into the Piazza Tasso, the main square in Sorrento and the focal-point of the town. It must be almost nine-thirty, she was sure, and, having parked her car in another hotel car park—the manager was a friend—she dodged between the never-ending stream of vehicles to reach the Caffè Fauno, the most popular meeting place in the town. All Sorrento life passed by the place, but today she was not really noticing the people around her. She turned her worried gaze over the tables and found Dante. He caught her eye and smiled, rising to his feet; she hurried towards him.

'Not so fast, Lexi,' a deep voice drawled in her ear as a strong hand closed firmly around her upper arm.

'What?' With sinking heart she looked up into the hard face of the man holding her. 'Jake,' she choked, her startled gaze skimming over his tall form. This morning he was dressed in cream chinos and a blue short-sleeve cotton shirt with a button-down collar, open at the neck to reveal the strong line of his throat and the beginnings of dark, curling chest hair.

'Take your hand off my fiancée.' Dante appeared in front of her, his deep brown eyes narrowed angrily on Jake, before flicking to Lexi. 'Are you all right, *cara*?' he asked, reaching to plant a kiss on her cheek.

Brutally, she was jerked out of Dante's reach, as Jake's arm closed around her waist like a band of steel. His eyes flashed with fury, and a muscle jerked in his cheek. 'Keep your hands and your mouth off my wife,' he said dangerously.

'Wife?' Dante's brows rose in surprise as his gaze slid from one to the other then settled on Jake. 'Not for much longer,' he responded firmly, reading the situation at a glance and grasping Lexi's other arm. 'So, this is why you wanted to see me so urgently, *cara*. Is he trying to cause trouble?' His dark eyes sought hers, puzzled but caring.

She felt like a rag doll pulled between the two bristling males, and, before she could open her mouth to speak, Jake spoke for her.

'I'll cause you trouble if you don't get your hand off my wife. It's over, and if I ever see you anywhere near Lexi again I will break every bone in your body. Understand?' There was no mistaking the deadly intent in Jake's tone and everyone at the surrounding tables was aware of it, never mind that it was in English.

Jake stood towering over Lexi and Dante, his dark face hard as rock, the venom in his eyes there for all to see.

Dante's hand dropped from her arm. 'What has happened, Lexi? Yesterday you said your divorce was only weeks away. You agreed to marry me.'

She could have wept. Dante did not deserve to be humiliated in public by the arrogant Jake.

Jake's fingers bit into her waist. 'Yes, tell him, Lexi darling. Tell him how you spent the night in my arms.'

'You didn't!' Dante cried, his eyes dark with pain, and, breaking into his native language, he demanded to know if she had slept with Jake.

Haltingly she tried to explain, but she could see Dante did not believe her as he turned on her in a fury of Italian, demanding to know why, when she had refused him her bed, she could fall straight into bed with a man she had not seen in years.

She looked into his deep brown eyes, and could see the hurt and anger and she opened her mouth to try and explain, and closed it again. There was no explanation she could give. It was better that Dante thought the worst of her; he would get over her quicker that way. Sadly she realised she had never loved him, and he deserved better.

'Jake is right, Dante. I'm sorry,' she said in English for Jake's benefit, but it hurt to see the look of bleak disillusionment on Dante's friendly face, and turning angry eyes on Jake, she added, 'Jake and I are reconciled—that's what you want, isn't it, darling...?' she jeered, not bothering to hide her disgust with her so-called husband.

Dante, with a pride that did him credit, said, 'Congratulations; I hope you will be happy, but I doubt it.' And, swinging on his heel, his broad shoulders tense, he walked stiffly away.

Lexi watched him go with tears in her eyes...

'He isn't worth your sympathy. The man is even older than me; he could never have kept you satisfied.'

Jake's sneering remark fuelled her temper, and flashing him a bitter glance, she said, 'Did you have to be so brutal? I wanted to tell Dante myself. And anyway, how did you know where to find us?'

'Simple, I went to the man's shop and followed him when he left; I guessed you would run to him. But you're wasting time, Lexi. Monicelli told me you spoke to him this morning; you have nowhere to run to. So, unless you want a coffee, we will leave.'

He was right as usual but she could not resist getting a dig at him. 'I'm surprised you don't need a coffee, given the state you got into last night; the place reeked of whisky this morning.' She tilted her head back, the better to look at him. 'Is drinking another one of your vices?' she queried sarcastically.

It wasn't natural, she thought bitterly; his deep blue eyes were as clear and cold as ice, and if he had a hangover it certainly didn't show. He looked more vitally alive today than he had yesterday.

'Sorry to disappoint you, my dear, but my head is fine and I am in full control of my faculties. I didn't drink the whisky last night so much as spill it down my trousers. Jet-lag was responsible for my oversleeping; I flew in from America yesterday morning.' His dark head bent towards her. 'Sorry you were frustrated last night, Lexi, but have no fear, I'll make it up to you,' he promised silkily, 'now I've deprived you of your lover.'

Her mouth fell open in shock and colour rushed into her face as the implication of his words hit her. 'I was not...'

'This is hardly the place to discuss your sex life,' he said sneeringly. 'Come along, my car is parked around the corner.'

'Come along? Where to?' She was not going to be manhandled like a piece of spare baggage, but she had no choice but to go where he led, the arm around her waist gripped even tighter as they walked from the café and down the Via Cesareo. 'And what about my car? I've left it at the Continental Hotel car park...'

'That will be taken care of—get in.'

Seated in the low passenger seat of the gleaming Bugatti, she flinched as Jake reached across her, the back of his knuckles brushing the tip of her breast as he fastened the seatbelt.

His deep blue eyes captured hers, and he was amused by her reaction; his hand dropped to cover her breast through the fine cotton of her shirt. 'So sensitive,' Jake prompted cynically. 'I did you a favour getting rid of Dante, he was no match for your fiery passion.'

She searched frantically for a scathing response, but Jake simply settled behind the wheel and started the car while she was still seething with anger. With a defiant toss of her head she looked out of the side window. She was not going to argue with the man, she wouldn't give him the satisfaction, and with hard-won control she offered, 'If you take the next left, it is the quickest way back to the hotel.'

Jake glanced sideways at her stiff face and then returned his attention to the road. 'We are not going to the hotel, but to my villa in Positano.'

Her head swung back, her glance going to his stern profile. 'But I can't; all my clothes, everything I own is at the hotel.'

'That's all taken care of. I'm taking no chances on your running off again,' he told her bluntly. 'I want you where I know you can't escape.'

Escape. It was an emotive word, but did one truly ever escape from one's past by running away? With maturity and hindsight, she recognised that her biggest mistake had been running away from Jake and his mistress in the first place. If she had stayed, and immediately applied for a divorce on the ground of Jake's adultery with Lorraine, she would certainly have won the case, the poor wife having just lost her child. Her solicitor had told her as much a couple of mornings ago. Not that it did her much good, as he also explained that, having been living apart for so long, to claim adultery now was a bit of a non-starter; it was best to wait the five years...

So near and yet so far, she thought, her violet eyes resentfully skimming Jake's harsh profile. She had almost won, a few short weeks to freedom. But almost was not good enough, she sighed resignedly; Jake always won... Her eyes fell on his hands lightly flexed around the wheel. He drove the powerful car with the same easy expertise he did everything. It was frightening to think she was completely at his mercy.

But five minutes later she was glad of his dynamic skills, as the powerful car picked up speed and flew along the notorious Amalfi Drive. She glanced out of the window and caught her breath: on one side were steeply rising cliffs, and on the other an almost sheer drop into the sea. It was noted as one of the most spectacular views in the Mediterranean, and many a film-maker used the scenic drive as a backdrop for famous car chases. But it took a skilful and courageous driver to navigate the dark tunnels and cliff-hanging bends. She didn't speak, didn't dare. Instead she drank in the sight of the isle of Capri, and the smaller islands near the coastline, the luxury yachts moving through the azure waters as smooth as swans on a lake.

Jake must have amassed an enormous amount of money to have a villa in Positano; she had visited the village once. A very sophisticated centre, the famous names in fashion owned the boutiques—Armani, Valentino and the like. Their customers the seriously rich people who holidayed in the villas dotted around the hillside. Roger Moore, the famous James Bond actor, and many more.

She gasped as the car swung violently to the right, and they were driving up a narrow road, and then, just when she thought they would surely crash into the tall iron gates ahead of them, Jake flicked a switch on the dash, and the gates swung open. A short, steep drive lined with trees ended in a huge stone arch and a large courtyard.

'My home—do you like it?' Jake was out of the car and holding the passenger door open for her.

Lexi, to put it crudely, was gobsmacked. She stepped out on to the paved yard, her violet eyes widened to their fullest extent. She gazed around her in awe. Gleaming white stucco with rough stone corners and arches—the villa was a work of art. Set into the hillside, long circular terraces curved around all three floors, a multitude of flowers and vines, hibiscus, and seemingly thousands of geraniums of every hue in huge ornate containers. It was how she imagined the hanging gardens of Babylon must have looked. She said nothing as Jake took her arm and led her up a wide stone staircase to the massive arched entrance door. The door was flung open and a small, dark-haired lady dressed completely in black burst into a voluble welcome in Italian.

Her footsteps halted in surprised astonishment as Jake returned the woman's greeting. 'I didn't know you spoke Italian.' She looked up into his smiling face, and was stunned by the obvious pleasure in his eyes at the sight of the old lady. Once Jake had looked at her like that. The thought stung, as the smile left his eyes when he turned his attention to her.

'There's a lot you don't know about me; you were never that interested.' Jake shrugged lazily, his broad shoulders flexing beneath his fine shirt.

He was right; when they were first married she had been too young, too much in awe of him to question him about anything, plus when they had been alone together they had spent most of their time in bed...

'Lexi, my housekeeper, Maria.'

Lexi with a start realised Jake was speaking, and, glad to banish the memories of the past, she took the older lady's outstretched hand in a brief handshake, but she got the distinct impression Maria was somewhat reluctant to accept her. She listened as Jake issued instruction for lunch to be served at one, and watched as Maria scuttled off to the back of the house, and Jake strode across the ornate marble mosaic floor to the foot of a large white marble staircase.

'Come along, Lexi.' A cool smile curved his hard mouth. 'I'm sure you want to get out of those clothes.' His dark eyes slid slowly over her face and throat, taking in the thrust of her breasts against the simple cotton shirt, the narrow waist and conservative straight skirt, and back up again to her face.

She felt as though he could see through to her flesh and she shivered, a sharp *frisson* of fear running down her spine, and stared at him in silence, incapable of responding.

Jake walked over to her. 'Your uniform is unnecessary here, Lexi; we are here to relax,' he said, and his long fingers closed over her chin and his thumb brushed along her bottom lip. 'And I am going to make you forget every man you ever looked at, except me.'

Lexi flushed, but there was no heat in Jake's eyes, she noted. She was looking at a stranger. His face was blank, hostile as he watched her; she felt the pressure of his fingers, the warmth of his body, and felt her throat tighten in fear.

'After you,' Jake drawled, and she heard the mockery in his tone as his hand dropped to curve around her back, propelling her forward.

Stiffly she moved towards the grand staircase. They climbed the stairs and walked down a wide corridor, their heels clicking like a death knell, Lexi thought fancifully, on the marble floors. Jake stopped at a door, opened it and urged her in. The room was bright and airy, flooded with the morning sun; the king-sized bed dominating it was covered with an intricate white lace bedspread.

'The master bedroom,' Jake drawled, and, going over to a door set in one plain white wall, he flung it open. 'Through here, the bathroom. The rest of this floor is taken up with another bedroom and the nursery suite. The top floor houses three more bedrooms and the service flat. The layout for the ground floor you can see for yourself later.'

'It's very nice,' she said politely. The room was obviously on the corner of the house, as two large windows were set in the wall to the right of her along with two long ceiling-to-floor windows that framed the huge bed. She walked across to the window directly in front of her and gasped.

The view was too beautiful for words. The tree-lined drive had disguised the exquisitely terraced gardens that marched down in row after row to end at what must be the edge of a cliff, and then the sea, glistening brilliant blue, the faint outline of Capri visible in the far distance. She let her gaze swing around in a shallow arc; to one side was visible the tiny port of Positano, the luxury yachts lying at anchor in the marina. It was picture-postcard-perfect. She clasped her hands together, suddenly nervous, as she felt Jake's presence behind her. She could sense the undercurrent of sexual tension in the air around them. A bedroom was far too intimate a place to be with Jake.

'How long have you owned this place?' She turned to look at him, hoping by her simple question to break the tension sizzling in the air.

He stared down at her, his dark eyes brooding. 'About a year.'

'Why buy here?' Had he wanted to be near her? the errant thought entered her mind.

'It was left to me by my father.'

She raised her brows. 'Your father? But I thought he died years ago.'

'Well, you thought wrong.' His blue eyes avoided hers, and for a second Lexi felt sympathy, until he added dismissively, 'And I have no wish to discuss it with you.'

She should have known better than to waste her sympathy on him, and, straightening her shoulders, she said, 'Yes, well . . . If you will excuse me.' She made to walk past him but was stopped as one long arm snaked out and curved around her waist, hauling her in hard against his body.

'Not so fast, Lexi.' His eyes darkened as he looked down at her. 'You owe me for this morning,' he said under his breath. 'No woman leaves my bed without my say-so.' She felt herself sway against him. 'And certainly not to run to another man.'

Lexi stared at him, and swallowed hard on the lump of fear that lodged in her throat. His blue-black eyes captured hers, and there was no mistaking the predatory animal look she saw in his dark face. 'I wasn't running away...'

'No...' he drawled mockingly. 'Then convince me...'

CHAPTER SIX

'No.' LEXI lifted her hands, intending to push him away, but his strong arm wrapped tighter around her small waist, his fingers biting into her side as he turned her fully in front of him, his long legs pressing against her slender limbs. Her hands came up against the hard wall of his chest; she could feel the steady beat of his heart beneath her fingers. The heat of his body, through the fine fabric of his shirt, burnt the palms of her hands, sending electric sensations shooting through her entire body.

'You want to, you know you do, Lexi. I saw it in those huge pansy eyes of yours last night when I kissed you. I could have taken you there and then,' Jake's deep voice husked beguilingly. 'Why deny yourself the pleasure?'

The horrible truth was she did want him. Held close against him, she could feel his rising awareness taut against her belly. But the mention of last night reminded her of her humiliation. She had come apart in his arms, only to hear him say she disgusted him ... She strained away from him but the action pulled her shirt taut across her firm breasts, without giving her the freedom she wanted. She could feel her pulse beat faster, the blood flowing thickly through her veins. She tilted her head back to look up into his darkly brooding face. 'I disgust you. You told me so. Why the change?' she queried, fighting to still the tremors curling her insides.

'I wasn't telling the whole truth; your mercenary nature I can do without,' he said with casual insolence as his indigo eyes slid from her upturned face to her breasts. 'But your body I want.'

She saw the darkening gleam in his gaze, and felt the subtle increase of pressure in his thighs. 'Well, I don't want you,' she croaked, her throat closing on the lie.

'Liar, you don't mean that.' And, holding her fast, he lifted his free hand to the buttons of her blouse and slowly unfastened them one by one, adding silkily, 'But perhaps you need *me* to convince you...'

Her violet eyes were trapped by the sensuous deepening gleam in Jake's, she knew she should stop him, but was paralysed by the hypnotic magnetism of the man. She felt boneless in the circle of his arm, her senses coming alive with every touch, every brush of his hard body.

His fingers quickly dealt with the front fastening of her bra, and her lush breasts broke free from their confinement as if leaping for his touch. 'You have developed into a very luscious lady, Lexi.'

She breathed a jagged breath, and tried again to push at his broad chest. 'Wasn't Lorraine enough for you this mor——?' she tried to strike back, but his strong hand closed over one naked breast, cupping the fullness, and words failed her.

'Forget about Lorraine; we have an agreement, you and I. Fidelity for the duration,' he drawled huskily as his thumb delicately grazed over the soft pink tip. 'And it won't be any hardship for either of us, if this is anything to go by, my darling *wife*.'

Lexi shuddered. He was seducing her with words and actions, and she had no defence against him.

'Look, Lexi, you do want me. See how this tempting pink bud aches for my touch,' his deep voice murmured sexily, as his fingers teased the rosy nub into pulsating rigidity.

She closed her eyes in shame, unable to bear the humiliation of knowing she had no control over her own body, as arrows of heat darted from her breast to her groin. She knew she should protest, but instead a soft moan escaped her.

'Don't close your eyes, Lexi. Look at me,' Jake commanded, his fingers nipping on the rigid tip of her breast.

She opened her eyes as liquid fire swirled through her, and glanced down. She saw his long, tanned fingers contrasting sharply with her soft, pale flesh, caressing, cajoling. It was madness, she hated Jake for what he had done to her, but it was a madness she could not resist. It had been too long...

'Tell me what you want, Lexi.' His hand stroked softly to the valley between her breasts then gently cupped the other one in his large palm, his forefinger tracing circles on her hardening flesh, but stopping well short of the hungry peak. 'Is this one feeling left out?' he teased sensuously as his dark head bent lower and his mouth closed over hers in the lightest brush of a kiss.

'Ask me nicely, Lexi, and I'll ease the ache for you...' he murmured, smiling wickedly as he watched her body arch instinctively towards him in helpless response.

Then his mouth once more closed over hers, his tongue slipping between her softly parted lips, and desire as sharp and piercing as a knife sliced through her. Her tongue touched his in thrusting response. She moaned as his fingers finally captured the taut nipple, tugging, rolling her between his sensitive fingertips; she raked her hands down his broad back, her lower body moving into him, pressing against him in a urgent need.

Jake raised his head, his dark eyes glittering triumphantly down into hers. 'You want me,' he grated 'Your body doesn't lie.' And his dark head swooped down to her aching breast and, as one hand caressed and teased her aching flesh, his mouth curved over its partner, nibbling, kissing then suckling long and slow until she thought she would go mad with pleasure.

'You're so responsive there, so ready for my mouth,' he rasped throatily as his dark head moved to her other breast. 'But we must make them both the same,' he chuckled, his mouth replacing his fingers, as he treated the rigid nipple to the same ecstasy as its partner.

Hardly aware of what she was doing, Lexi's hands crept up his spine to the nape of his neck, her fingers tangling in the dark hair of his head, holding him against her. She never noticed as he swept her up in his arms and carried her to the bed, because his mouth covered hers in an all-consuming kiss of passionate intent, his tongue plunging into her mouth, seeking to devour all the hot, sweet taste of her.

She felt the mattress at her back as Jake eased his mouth from hers, and, sliding on to the bed at her side, he deftly removed her blouse and bra, his hand stroking from her throat, his palm caressing over her full breasts, first one and then the other.

'Jake...' she murmured his name. Her tongue licking out over her swollen lips, she stared up into his handsome face; his mouth was a taut line in a face flushed dark with desire.

'Yes, Lexi...' he rasped, one hand sliding her skirt down over her slender hips. 'I'm going to make it so good for you.'

Jake's mouth brushed a soft kiss from the hollow in her throat down the valley of her breast. He lifted his dark head and looked slowly from her beautiful passion-flushed face to the wild mass of red hair spread across the pillow, like molten gold gleaming in the rays of morning sun cutting across the huge bed. His sensuous gaze slowly traced the thrust of her naked breasts, hard and pouting for his touch, the soft curve of her waist and gentle flare of her hips. His hand slid beneath the fine lace of her briefs and eased them down her shapely legs.

Lexi shivered uncontrollably, aching to feel his naked flesh. Her rational mind knew he was deliberately se-ducing her in broad daylight, but it had been so long . . . She reached up to his chest, her fingers fumbling with the fastening of his shirt.

'Let me,' Jake grated and, pushing her hands away, quickly shrugged out of his clothes.

Lexi's violet eyes skimmed his golden body, gloriously naked stretched alongside her, the dark swirls of chest hair arrowing down past his flat stomach, the curve of his buttock, the long, muscular legs. Five years had only enhanced his male perfection, she thought wonderingly. She reached her small hands up to his chest, her slender fingers weaving in his body hair, finding the hard male nipples. She smiled, a slow, sensual curve of her mouth, as she tweaked the rigid little nubs.

Jake groaned deep in his throat and pushed her hands away yet again. Leaning over her, he spread her arms either side of her head, and his dark eyes burned down into hers—passion, desire, she saw them all, and something else besides that slowed her rapidly beating heart.

'I've waited five long years for this moment,' he growled huskily.

He was lying; five years ago he hadn't wanted her, couldn't get rid of her fast enough. The errant thought flickered in Lexi's head, but vanished as his lips brushed against her brow in the lightest caress.

'I've dreamed of having your exquisite body pinned beneath me, of making you cry out my name once more, begging me to take you, and I will not be hurried, my darling Lexi.'

The drawled endearment should have enthralled her, but instead a quiver of fear pierced the sensual haze swamping her mind. Jake flung one long leg over her trembling limbs, holding her fast, his soft body hair, the hard heat of his arousal pushed against her thigh and she half closed her eyes, fear forgotten, at the lightning speed at which her body shook with want and need.

Through the thick fringe of her lashes she saw Jake's harsh face lower to within inches of her own. Her lips parted for his kiss.

'I am going to make love to you——' his lips moved against her mouth and away again '—until every other man who ever had you is banished from your mind. Until the only name you ever cry is mine. My magnificent, mercenary little wife.'

'Mercenary...?' she murmured. He had called her that before...

'That and more, but I can forget it all when I have sated myself in you.'

Lexi's eyes widened to their fullest extent as she gazed up into his taut features and she trembled at what she saw there, in the stark, bright morning light. It wasn't love, not even lust, but something more sinister...

Dazed with passion, she tried to think. Mercenary...he kept harping on that and yet she had never taken a penny from him. Then, with a flash of insight, she remembered their parting in London; she had pretended, to save her pride in the face of his infidelity, that she would rather have half his wealth than him. She smiled, and opened her mouth to reassure him.

'Jake...' She stopped herself just in time. If she explained why she had acted mercenary, he would realise just how much he had hurt her, how much she had loved him! It was the last coherent thought she had for a long time...

'Yes, Lexi; I know.' And releasing her hands, he stroked the length of her arms, the curve of her breast and her flat stomach; his strong hands curved over her hips, his long fingers trailing towards her inner thighs, but not lingering as they stroked right down to her feet and back up again.

Her heartbeat accelerated like a rocket. She felt how a cat must feel being stroked; she wanted to purr, and rub herself against the source of the pleasure. She clasped her hands around his broad shoulders, her body arching, writhing against his in wanton invitation.

'Easy,' Jake said, his voice ragged. He looked down at her sensuously flushed face, the softly parted lips. 'I'll give you what you want.' His dark head lowered and he was kissing her swiftly, repeatedly, on her mouth, her eyes, the slender line of her throat. 'I'm glad you haven't lost all modesty,' Jake murmured lifting his head. His dark eyes gleamed down into hers. 'There are a few interesting white triangles here.' One long finger traced the soft curve of her breast. 'A mathematician could have a field-day working out the angles,' he husked as he bent his head, his tongue tracing the slight outline in her flesh where her bikini top had left its mark, then, cutting across, his tongue laved the burgeoning tips of her breasts.

Lexi moaned her need, her mouth sought him, she kissed the back of his hand, biting on his forearm that lay across her breast-bone, holding her down. The taste of him was in her mouth, the male scent of him filled her nostrils; she was lost in a sea of tempestuous emotions she had thought never to experience again. Her hands grasped his hard flesh, clinging to his broad shoulders; her nails dug into his satin-smooth skin as he licked and kissed his way down her body.

She was aflame; everywhere he touched was transformed into million points of pleasure. His long fingers found the third curling red triangle, and she cried out his name, 'Jake...'

He looked into her face as one strong hand gently urged her legs apart, opening her to his final possession, while his fingers stroked erotically. She watched his eyes darken to black pools, and he was shaking with the same wild desire that consumed her.

It was as if her body had been in prison for five years and was suddenly given its freedom. She was free to experience everything, to relish once more Jake claiming her, but he didn't. His dark head bent and she quivered from head to toe as his touch, his tongue, became so intimate she thought she would die. She felt the tremors start in the heart of her womb, the tendrils reaching in ever widening circles.

Jake slid up her body, his mouth finding hers, his teeth and tongue biting and tasting her full pouting lips. 'You're hot, so hot,' he murmured, as his hand slid between her thighs, tangling in the soft, red curls and finding the soft, feminine folds again.

She trembled wildly on the brink while Jake looked down at her, his smile a mixture of savage triumph and fiercely held control.

'Tell me what you want, Lexi.' His fingers stroked.

She reached for him, needing his weight, his body over her, in her, as red-hot need scorched her innermost being.

'Say it, Lexi,' he growled, his deep voice shaking as he lifted himself into the cradle of her thighs.

He wanted it all; Jake wanted her to beg. She hated him, but desire overwhelmed her. The brush of the hard hot length of him against her was too much. 'Jake, I want you.' Her voice broke as her love-starved body quivered like a bow. She arched up to him, her shapely legs curving around his thighs. 'Please, Jake...'

Jake rubbed against her again but stopped just at the edge of taking her. 'You do it, Lexi. Convince me, lover...'

Her deep purple eyes clashed with Jake's. His skin was pulled taut over his high cheekbones; his dark eyes glittered with a violent light as he fought to control his own need. He brushed lightly against her once more, teasing, almost penetrating and with a sigh of surrender she gave him the triumph he demanded. Her hand slid eagerly between their sweat-slicked bodies, her fingers crawling over his flat belly and lower, finding the satin-sheathed steel of him. He jerked reflexively, and there was no need for guidance as he drove deeply into her.

Lexi's hands curved around his back, clinging as he drove deep and deeper; their bodies, hot, wet and wanting, moved in frenzied rhythm. Lexi felt the widening circles flinging her out into infinity, breaking in wave after wave of tumultuous relief. She sobbed his name, then his mouth ground down on hers, as, with one final thrust of body and tongue, Jake shuddered over the edge into oblivion with her.

'I'm too heavy for you,' Jake's rasping voice declared prosaically, and, rolling off her, he lay flat on his back, an arm flung across his eyes, as if shutting out the light.

Lexi glanced at him, his great chest heaving in the aftermath of passion, but the space he had put between them was more eloquent than words. 'Jake?' she queried, reaching out to him.

'No inquest, Lexi. You enjoyed it as much as me,' he drawled callously, not even bothering to look at her.

She briefly closed her eyes against the shame while admitting that Jake was right as usual. They had made love countless times in the past; it was nothing new, she told herself. But never had she felt so totally possessed. She tried to convince herself it was just good sex. She was more mature and could accept it as such, after all, he was her husband! Why not? That excuse was the most pathetic of all, and she knew it.

Jake sat up, and, glancing sideways at her naked sprawled body, his gaze finally rested on her face. 'You wanted me, Lexi! Thanks! You convinced me most satisfactorily.' His lips quirked in a mocking smile. 'I think we will get along just fine.' And, swinging his long legs off the bed, totally happy with his nudity, he walked around the room collecting his clothes.

Lexi flinched as though he had struck her, unable to respond. Five years' abstinence had been ended by Jake's sophisticated expertise in the art of making love. He had done it quite deliberately, reduced her to a mindless wanton in his arms. Before, she had believed Jake's lovemaking was the ultimate expression of his love for her, until she had caught him with Lorraine... Now he had demonstrated graphically that his lovemaking had nothing whatsoever to do with love, but everything to do with possession, ownership. Jake decided he wanted her back, for whatever devious reason, and dismissed the past five years of her life as though they had never existed. Bed the woman! Back to the status quo! Reconciled! Jake was right, she had wanted him, but now, looking at him strolling around the bedroom all arrogant, smug, self-satisfied male, she wished she'd castrated the swine.

'I need a shower, and then I have some work to take care of in the study.' Jake stopped with his hand on the bathroom door and glanced to where she lay as he had left her, naked on the bed.

Lexi met his gaze. 'I really do hate you,' she said bleakly, and she hated herself, she recognised sadly. The bright morning sun filled the room, exposing every minute detail; it was barely noon and she had... She couldn't bear to think of it! Grabbing the edge of the lace bedspread, she pulled it up over her naked body.

'Bit late for that, sweetheart, I've seen it all and more.' His masculine chuckle only added to her humiliation. 'I can have you any time I want and after this morning's little romp we both know it.'

His arrogant assumption was all it took to ignite Lexi's anger and, hauling herself upright on the bed with the cover firmly clasped above her breast, she recalled his words of the previous night. 'So much for waiting to make sure any offspring were definitely yours,' she lashed back defiantly.

For a moment she watched his eyes narrow assessingly on her small face, and then a cynical smile twisted his firm mouth. 'I don't need to, Lexi; your boyfriend was most forthcoming this morning. You forget, I speak Italian.'

She groaned inwardly as she realised Jake must have understood every word of Dante's angry speech earlier. Jake knew Dante had never been her lover. But still, she snapped back mutinously, 'You don't know everything.'

An expression of cold derision tautened his handsome face. 'I don't want to; your body in my bed when I say so is enough.' And opening the bathroom door he added as an afterthought, 'Your luggage arrived earlier from the hotel. Maria has put it in the room next door. Don't forget, lunch at one on the patio. Maria doesn't like to be kept waiting.'

Lexi bent her head, her hands curling into fists. Her fingers bit painfully into her soft palms, but it was nothing to the pain she felt inside. Silently she raged at Jake, at the circumstances that had put her here in his bed, and most of all at herself. You're a fool, a weak-willed sex-starved idiot! she told herself bitterly, and, worse, she had the sinking feeling she had let herself in for a world, possibly a lifetime, of pain.

Abruptly rolling off the bed, Lexi stood up, letting the coverlet fall back behind her; action might dispel her unwelcome thoughts. Quickly she searched for her clothes and, picking them up, she slipped on her briefs then winced as she fastened her bra; her breasts were still tender from Jake's ministrations.

Jake! Her nemesis! He couldn't have made it plainer. He would use her when and where he wanted to, and she had to jump to his order. She tried to tell herself she was glad that at least Jake was allowing her to have her own bedroom, but, as she wriggled into her skirt and blouse, and walked across the room to the door, deep in the secret part of her heart, that hurt most of all...

She walked along the corridor, and pushed open the partially opened door of what she presumed was the next room and looked in. Her eyes fell on her battered suit-cases standing just inside the door; she heaved a sigh of relief and walked in, closing the door behind her.

Lexi found herself standing in a small, arched alcove. She stepped forward and for the first time in ages her generous mouth curved in the beginnings of a smile as she looked around. The room was a delight; a symphony in gold, cream and the palest lavender.

The walls either side of her were a bank of mirrored wardrobes, which accounted for the small arched entrance-hall. On the wall to the left was a four-poster bed draped in yards of cream eyelet lace lined with lavender silk; a matching cover lay over the bed. Opposite her, two long windows were hung with complementary curtains, caught back at the sides by models of Eros in gold to reveal the terrace and breathtaking view beyond. Between the windows was a huge mirror in an amethyst frame, and in front of that, a deliciously feminine chaiselongue and matching button-backed chair, plus a circular glass and gold occasional table. On the right-hand side wall was a long kneehole dressing-table, draped in the same fabric, with a three-way mirror on top, and next to that was another door.

It was the most totally feminine room Lexi had ever seen, and it all looked new. A variety of pictures dotted the walls, from old-fashioned landscapes to a Gainsborough lady in a velvet frame, and they were all fixed with satin bows and suspended on ribbons. A couple of Aubusson rugs were placed at strategic points on the marble tiled floor.

She crossed the room, her handbag catching her attention; she hadn't realised she had left it in the car. It rested, along with a small leather box, on the dressing-table. Maria had been thorough. It was Lexi's jewel-box, not that she had much jewellery, but flicking it open she drew out her wristwatch and slipped it on; she had forgotten it in her haste to get away from Jake that morning. Not that it had done her any good, she sighed wearily. Her hand hovered over the box and slowly, reluctantly, she moved aside a few pieces of jewellery to reveal a plain gold ring. She hadn't looked at it in years, but she had never quite got around to throwing it away.

Lexi picked up the gold band and held it in the palm of her hand, such a simple piece of jewellery that had once meant the world to her. In her mind's eye she saw herself as a young girl walking into the register office on the arm of Meg's husband Tom. She had been nervous, but it had been a trembly, exciting kind of nerves. Her wedding-dress had been a delicate white *broderie anglaise* affair. Jake had insisted she must wear white, the same way after only a couple of dates he had discovered she was a virgin and insisted she marry him. At the time she had thought it was because he loved her and had too much respect for her to indulge in an affair.

With hindsight, she realised grimly, it had simply been a very smart move on his part to acquire Forest Manor and turn it into a hotel. True, he had paid her father's debts and made her a sleeping partner in his business, in fact he had insisted on it. She smiled drily; for all she knew she might be a very wealthy woman in her own right by now. She had had no contact with the London merchant bank where Jake had opened her account since the day he had taken her there to sign the necessary documents.

'You kept it. That does surprise me.'

Lexi jumped as if she had been stung, and whirling round her startled eyes clashed with cold blue. 'Do you have to creep up on people like that?' she burst out; she had not heard him approach, and she blushed scarlet, embarrassed and angry with herself.

'I did not creep, as you put it.' His cool eyes looked mockingly down at her. 'But you were so lost in thought that you didn't hear me. Pleasant memories, were they?' he probed, his hand reaching out and curving around her closed palm, forcing her fingers to open.

Lexi was incapable of responding with his unexpected presence only a few inches in front of her. The touch of his hand had set her heart racing and the image of what had happened earlier in his bedroom leapt to the forefront of her mind.

'Too simple for your taste. I imagined you had consigned it to the rubbish bin years ago.'

'Wh-what..?' Wide-eyed, she stared at him, her thoughts in chaos. His lips parted over even white teeth in a grin of genuine amusement at her obvious confusion. 'Never mind. It'll do until I get you a diamond one.' And with casual arrogance he took the gold band and slipped it on her ring finger, and she let him, too surprised to do anything else.

'Still a perfect fit. Just like you and I, Lexi.'

She stared at him, the colour flooding her face at his words. 'So you say,' she tried to jeer, but it was right, he had proved it very thoroughly not half an hour ago. She glanced down at their joined hands, anything to avoid Jake's too knowing expression, but the gold ring glittering on her finger only served to remind her of the hopelessness of her position, and swiftly she pulled her hand free.

Jake lifted her chin with one long finger. 'Don't look so shocked,' he chuckled. 'We are married.' And, trailing his finger up to her lips, he added softly but with deadly intent, 'And this time you will not escape. Which brings me to why I'm here.'

'I thought you had work to do,' Lexi said, finally finding the control to string a sentence together.

'True, but first your passport.'

'My passport...'

'Yes, it wasn't at the hotel and I want it.'

She glanced sideways at where her bag lay on the dressing-table, and Jake, intercepting her glance, swiftly picked up the bag and opened it.

Seeing Jake rummaging around in her bag was the incentive Lexi needed to find her pride and her temper. 'Put that down, damn you,' she demanded and, stepping forward, reached up to grab it. 'You have no right to go through my personal belongings.' She jumped up, trying to catch Jake's hand holding her bag, but only succeeded in losing her balance and falling hard against his broad chest. A long arm snaked around her waist pinning her to his side while the bag dropped to the floor, but she saw her precious passport firmly clenched in his fist, way out of her reach.

'Now, now, Lexi, don't get excited.' She heard his chuckle and saw red.

'Give me that.' She kicked out at his shin and futilely tried to reach his outstretched arm.

She almost fell over as Jake abruptly released her, his dark eyes turned from her open passport to her furious face.

'So that's how you did it. I should have guessed,' he said harshly, all amusement gone. 'Miss Alexandra Laughton.' He read her name as if it was a dirty word. 'You never did get this changed.'

She stared up at him, her violet eyes simmering with anger. But his embittered gaze made her bite back her angry demand. He looked ready to do violence and she didn't understand why, but a fine-honed sense of self-protection had her stepping backwards until she could go no further, the wall at her back.

Jake followed her, his large body tense like a coiled spring, his rugged features taut with barely controlled anger. His strong hands shot out and rested heavily on her slender shoulders. He pushed his dark face to within inches of her own.

'My God, you had it planned all along,' he hissed, his breath grazing her face. His dark eyes studied her, taking in the smooth forehead, the delicately arched eyebrows, the soft curve of her cheek.

Lexi's tongue snaked out over her dry lips in a nervous gesture, her heart thudding in her breast; a violent tension hung in the air between them, and she didn't know how it had happened.

'Such a beautiful, innocent face disguising a viciously devious mind.' Jake shook his dark head, his hands falling from her shoulders.

'That's rich...' Lexi stopped as her wary gaze clashed with Jake's, and what she saw in the black depths froze the blood in her veins.

'You have a good right to look afraid, Lexi, but right at this moment I don't think I could bear to touch you, or if I did I would strangle you.' And spinning around he stormed out of the room.

Long after he left Lexi was still leaning against the wall; she did not trust her legs to carry her one step. She had never seen Jake so furious or such hatred in another human being's face in her life. Slowly recovering her self-control, she pushed herself away from the wall and crossed the short space to the chaise-longue and collapsed upon it.

What did Jake mean, she had planned? Instead of ranting simply because she had never got around to changing her passport, he should have been thanking her. Five years ago it had enabled Lexi to walk away, leaving Jake and his mistress with her old home and a clear field... The man was obviously unbalanced...

As for a devious plan, that was laughable. Lexi had rarely planned anything in her life. It was one of her failings, she freely admitted. She tended to be a creature of impulse; she had married Jake on little more than an impulse. She had left England in the same impulsive manner, when, if she had stayed and fought, she could have been a free woman now. Instead of which, she was caught in a nightmare of a marriage where both parties hated each other's guts.

Jake had accused her of being devious. What a joke— if any one was devious it was Jake. He had married her for the manor; true, he had paid her father's debt, but

she was sure it could not have been anything like the
amount of money Jake intended making with the hotel.
He had got her pregnant by mistake; he had not wanted
a child. A tear slid down her cheek. Five years ago this
very day Lexi had lain in the hospital bed having miscarried their child, and Jake had turned up hours after
the event with a few lame excuses about business for
neglecting Lexi. Now he turned up again, this time demanding a child, and with Lorraine, his mistress, in tow
to take care of Lexi's job, while presumably Lexi obliged
her husband. The black irony of the situation was too
much to bear.

Collapsing on the chaise-longue, she gave way to her
shattered emotions, tears of self-pity gushing down
her cheeks.

CHAPTER SEVEN

LEXI rolled over and fell with a thump on the floor. Her eyes flew open and for a second she wondered where she was. Struggling out of what felt like a strait jacket but was in reality a light cotton sheet, she sat up cross-legged on the floor and gazed around her as the events of the morning filled her mind. She sighed, rubbing her elbow where it had caught the carved-wood frame of the front of the chaise-longue; it was an elegant piece of furniture but not the best place to fall asleep, she thought ruefully, her eyes widening as she realised someone must have come in her room and put the sheet over her. Not that it was necessary; she felt hot and sweaty and longed for a bath. She glanced at her wristwatch and jumped to her feet in shock. It was almost four. Jake had said lunch at one...

With a toss of her head she stalked across to the door set in the wall by the dressing-table. She had missed lunch, but what the hell! Jake could hardly kill her for it, and she badly needed to find the bathroom. Opening the door, her lips parted in a smile of pleasure, as she looked around the exquisitely appointed bathroom. Her smile vanished when she caught sight of herself in the length of one mirrored wall. God, what a mess! Her hair was sticking out like a bush, her eyes were red-rimmed and her clothes were wrinkled beyond belief.

Five minutes later, stripped naked, she stood in the huge double shower; her muscles ached in places she had forgotten she possessed and dark smudges marred her smooth flesh, telling their own story, but under the relaxing influence of the warm soothing spray she slowly felt the ache and tension drain out of her. She washed her hair with a sweet-scented jasmine shampoo, one she had chosen from a good selection displayed on the vanity-unit alongside the circular bath. She had toyed with the idea of having a bath but after seeing the size of it decided it would probably take half an hour to fill, and, much as she told herself she didn't care about missing lunch, she could not ignore the pangs of hunger rumbling in her stomach for much longer.

Stepping out of the shower, blinking the water from her eyes, she stretched out a hand to where she thought the towel might be and was relieved to find it. With her head bent she dried the water from her eyes then swept the towel up around her hair in a turban. Throwing her head back, she straightened and froze with her hands at the knot in the towel.

Jake was standing in front of her, his blue eyes dancing with amusement as he took in her shocked expression, and quite a lot more besides.

'Very nice.' His gaze slid slowly down her naked body, lingering on her full breasts, and before she realised what he was doing he leant forward, his mouth catching the tip of her breast.

She lashed out at his dark head, stepping back, trying to ignore the flash of tingling awareness lancing through her body. 'Get out,' she cried and, swinging round, she grabbed a large white bath sheet from a nearby towel-rail and wrapped it hastily around her heated body.

'I couldn't resist catching the drop of water from your breast, Lexi, there's no need to throw a fit,' he drawled with mocking amusement.

Lexi did not share his amusement; she was flustered and furious, and the last thing she needed was his intimidating presence looming over her in the bathroom. She glared at him; it was positively wicked how attractive Jake looked, she thought bitterly. Some time in the past few hours he had changed into a pair of brief white shorts, and sleeveless white T-shirt. His long, muscular limbs, bronzed by the sun, were enough to make her heart flutter. 'I expect privacy in the bathroom. Surely that isn't too much to ask?' she demanded furiously.

'You're obviously feeling better. You have your temper back.'

'I wasn't ill, I fell asleep.' She tried to explain her absence from lunch before he could ask.

'I know; I called in earlier and you looked so peaceful that I put a cover over you and left. See how kind I can be when you please me,' Jake prompted with a knowing reminiscent curve to his hard mouth.

So it had been Jake! Somehow it did not fit her image of the ruthless man who had burst back into her life so suddenly. 'Thank you...' she muttered reluctantly. 'But if you don't mind I'd like to get dressed.'

'Don't let me stop you.' And in an exaggerated gesture he flung open the bathroom door. 'After you.'

It was hard to look dignified wrapped in a bath sheet with a towel round one's hair, but Lexi gave it her best shot and marched past him with her head held high, while silently mumbling, 'Arrogant swine' under her breath.

'I thought you might be hungry, so I had Maria prepare a tray, a few sandwiches and a pot of coffee.'

Lexi didn't want to acknowledge his thoughtfulness. 'You needn't have bothered; I'm not hungry,' she denied and, walking across the room, she sat down on the button-backed chair, casually eyeing the food set before her on the occasional table. 'You're enough to make any woman lose her appetite,' she added for good measure, but just at that moment her tummy gave a very loud rumble.

Jake tossed back his dark head and burst out laughing, and Lexi's lips began to twitch and, before she could help it, a chuckle escaped her. She looked up at Jake

standing a few feet away and, as blue eyes caught violet
in shared humour, the laughter stopped. Lexi could not
break the contact, and for a long moment something
precious seemed to simmer in the air between them.

Jake looked away first. 'Eat, Lexi, and meet me
downstairs in half an hour,' he commanded gruffly and,
turning on his heel, walked out.

Twenty minutes later, the food long gone, Lexi's lips
pursed thoughtfully as she surveyed her reflection. She
looked slightly better, she thought; her eyes were no
longer red-rimmed but the dark circles beneath betrayed
the stress of the last twenty-four hours. She had chosen
a soft cotton sleeveless shirtwaister in mint-green from
her limited but classic wardrobe, surprised to find everything she possessed had been neatly put away, probably
by Maria, including her shoes, neatly lined up in the
rack at the bottom of the wardrobe. She had picked a
pair of comfortable espadrilles in matching green; a trip
to the chest of drawers alongside the dressing-table and
she had found her underwear. Now, as she brushed her
hair back into a neat ponytail, fastening it with a plain
green slide, she knew she could not put off much longer
going downstairs, and Jake...

She need not have worried... Lexi carried the tray
that had held her snack down the grand staircase and,
presuming the kitchen was at the back of the house, made
her way through the hall to the door at the rear. Opening
it, she walked into a huge light and airy room. A large
antique pine dresser on one wall, stacked with blue delft
china, caught her eye; in the centre of the room was a
solid square pine table surrounded with ladder-backed
chairs, and beyond the table a dividing bench to the
kitchen proper. Maria, hearing Lexi enter, dashed across
to meet her and take the tray from her.

'*Signora*, please you should not have bothered. It is
my job to collect the tray, cook everything... What will
Signor Taylor say?'

Lexi smiled at the older woman's worried frown. 'Don't worry, Maria; I am quite capable of looking after myself.'

'But it is my job,' Maria said firmly, and she placed the tray on the bench.

Lexi caught the housekeeper's disapproving look and sighed inwardly. Not a very good start, she thought hopelessly, missing lunch and upsetting the housekeeper. 'Sorry,' she apologised. 'But if you tell me where I can find Mr Taylor, I'll get out of your way.'

'Signor Taylor left fifteen minutes ago. He will be back for dinner at eight. Do you wish to eat in the diningroom or outside, *signora*?'

So much for his instruction to meet him in thirty minutes; obviously something more important had caught his attention—probably Lorraine. Lexi sighed and glanced out of the window, the fierce heat of the sun did not seem to have diminished since the morning. 'Outside, thank you, Maria.' Anyway, it would be less intimate to eat outside, she told herself and, turning, left the room.

She spent the next half-hour exploring her new home. In any other circumstances she would have found the place delightful. An elegant dining-room opened out on to a sunny patio, and the kitchen at one side of the house. A morning-room and what she presumed was Jake's study led out to the terrace at the front of the house, as did the extravagantly furnished salon, the imposing entrance-hall bracketed between them. The salon opened on two sides to the terraces. Strolling through the tall French windows, she found herself at the other side of the house. She walked on the edge of the terrace and, looking over, gasped. On the next level down was a freeshaped swimming-pool, the clear water sparkling in the late afternoon sun. She toyed with the idea of going for a swim, but she had no intention of allowing Jake to catch her in her bikini; she was far too vulnerable to his masculine charms, though it infuriated her to have to admit it.

Instead she wandered down the stone steps to the pool, and on down through half a dozen progressively narrower terraces cascading with flowers and vines, the warm, sweet smell of a variety of plants filling the air, and beyond the boundary wall the magnificent backdrop of the sea, and islands. It was a little bit of paradise, Lexi mused, casually leaning against the wall, her eyes skimming the perfect view. But to her, short of diving off the cliff, it was a prison...

Restlessly she turned and slowly began walking back up towards the house. How long did Jake intend to keep her here? He was a businessman based in the city of London, it didn't make sense, but ruefully she admitted that nothing in the past twenty-four hours had made much sense. His demanding she return to him and his desire for a child were a puzzle she could not fathom. Jake had hardly been ecstatic the one time she had been pregnant; only weeks after her pregnancy had been confirmed, suddenly he had needed to work in London—pressure of business, he had told Lexi. That was a laugh. Pressure from his mistress, more like, as Lexi had so suddenly and painfully discovered.

Lexi would never forget the first meal she had shared with Jake and Lorraine after losing her baby, and the other woman's callous comment, 'You wouldn't have much time for a child just now... it might be a blessing in disguise.' With hindsight Lexi realised what Lorraine had been getting at. Jake must have already decided to end their marriage, and was just waiting for a convenient time to tell his poor little wife. A child would have been a complication Jake didn't need. It made Lexi's blood boil to think of the pair of them still together five years later almost to the day, and once more wrecking her life.

She stopped as she reached the edge of the swimming-pool, and closed her eyes, clasping her hands in front of her as though in prayer. Why, why, why hadn't Jake gone ahead with the divorce she had heard him and Lorraine plotting all those years ago? Her violet eyes fluttered open and she stared down into the sparkling blue water as if it would give her the answer she sought... It could only be money...

Lexi, as far as she knew, was still a silent partner in his business. Maybe he was frightened that if she divorced him he would lose half his business, yet she had tried to reassure him on that point last night. But he insisted on believing she was mercenary. Lorraine had once tried to convince Jake Lexi was a gold-digger before they were married, and obviously now Jake believed her. It appeared the other woman had overplayed her hand. The very reason Lorraine had given for Jake not marrying Lexi in the first place was now preventing Jake from divorcing Lexi... It would be laughable if it wasn't so tragic. God, her heart cried, wasn't it enough that she had lost her beloved baby, given Jake and Lorraine a clear field; what had she done to deserve their continued persecution?

Bending down at the edge of the pool, she ran her hand through the cool water and brushed it over her hot forehead. It must be financial, it was the only motive that made sense. But there was something else, she was sure of it. Male ego. Pride maybe. Jake didn't like the idea of Lexi finding someone else.

But was it that simple? She didn't know. The Jake who had stormed back into her life was vastly different from the man she had married. She could see it in his eyes, hear it in the scathing comments he voiced, and feel it in the almost palpable hatred that flared between them. Sadly for her, passion flared between them with the same if not greater force and to her constant shame she was incapable of withstanding the force of Jake's desire. No, not desire! Lust... and that self-knowledge was the most shaming of all.

Straightening, she glanced at the ring on her finger, once a symbol of eternal love, or so she had thought, now a cold band of possession, nothing more. Sadly she took the last few steps to the house.

She walked back into the salon and, collapsing on an over-stuffed sofa, she glanced around. Very elegant, the furniture, a mixture of antique and modern Italian, was complemented by a selection of exquisite porcelain and bronze statuettes, a huge ornate marble fireplace with a magnificently carved over-mirror, everything in the best taste.

She sighed. Her job had been her life for years; she was not used to being idle. She had gone to college with no great career ambition, but had assumed she would end up as a translator in the foreign office. Marrying Jake and getting pregnant had changed all that. She supposed in a way she had Jake to thank for her career in hotel management. It was an occupation she loved. She had discovered that she had a flair for adminis-tration and she enjoyed meeting a wide variety of people, but it looked very much as if the career Jake had given her he had ruthlessly taken away from her again.

Restless and ill at ease in the quiet splendour of the salon, she let her glance settle on the telephone on a small table by the fireplace. Leaping to her feet she crossed and picked it up dialling the number of the Piccolo Paradiso. She had every right to check up on her job, never mind that Lorraine was now in charge. Plus she felt guilty disappearing the way she had, even though it wasn't her fault. She should have rung earlier to make sure everything was running smoothly, and she would have done if Jake had not swept her into his bed. She squashed the quick flush of remembered pleasure, as Anna's voice echoed down the line.

'*Pronto. Le Piccolo Paradiso.*'

It was great to hear a familiar voice. 'Anna, it's me, Lexi—I——' Before she could finish her sentence Anna cut in, her voice bubbling with excitement.

'Aren't you the dark horse? All this time you had a husband, and what a husband! He's gorgeous. I can't think why you ever left him. But it's so romantic him finding you again, it made me cry——'

'You've met Jake...?' Lexi cut in, not in the least interested in the younger girl's romantic fairy-tale image of him.

'Of course, he was here this afternoon for a staff briefing. There are going to be a few changes, but he congratulated us all on our hard work for Mr Monicelli and hoped we would work as well for him. Wasn't that nice? And guess what? I'm the new senior receptionist, and Franco, after two weeks' training with the new computer Mr Taylor is having installed, is going to take over from Miss Lorraine as the manager.'

'Yes, very nice,' Lexi managed to get out, silently seething; obviously she was not indispensable, quite the reverse if Anna was to be believed, and that hurt... 'So, everything is going smoothly, no problems?' she couldn't help asking.

'You're not to worry about anything, Lexi, just relax and enjoy your gorgeous husband. I know I would if I were you. In fact, he's here again now, I've just sent coffee into the office for him and Miss Lorraine. Do you want me to put you through?'

'No,' Lexi snapped, 'it doesn't matter. I'll be in touch.' And she dropped the receiver into the cradle.

She wished she had never telephoned. Her pale lips tightened at the way Jake had so quickly organised her life, cutting her off from her career and her friends with ruthless efficiency. She stood up and walked slowly back out on to the terrace. She thrust her hands into the pockets of her dress, and strolled around the terrace, her head bent, lost in her own thoughts; she didn't notice the magnificent sunset. Jake was playing havoc with her life, her emotions, and she could see no way out. The fact that he had dashed straight back to Lorraine she tried to dismiss from her mind but it was there like a gnawing cancer eating at her self-esteem, her pride. Jake had destroyed her trust years ago and agreement or not, she did not trust him to be faithful to her. Had he found time to bed his mistress this afternoon? she wondered. Or maybe that was what he was doing now.

Suddenly a flash of light startled her and she jumped, her heart thudding. She sighed and looked around, surprised to notice that she had walked right around the house, and it was dark. The outside lanterns had switched on. For a long moment she gazed around. Lights glowed in the trees, illuminating the flowers and shrubs. She turned her head towards the house and outside the kitchen was a white wrought-iron dining-table surrounded by half a dozen chairs. Soft cushions in pink and blue picked up the colour of a huge parasol with an exquisite Chinese lantern suspended from its centre. A few comfortable loungers were spread around in front of the dining-room window along with a low table. As she watched, Maria bustled out on to the terrace, a loaded tray in her hand.

'Can I help?' Lexi asked.

'No, *signora*,' Maria declared disappearing back through the patio door into the kitchen.'

Lexi sighed and sat down on the nearest lounger. Lying back against the soft cushions, she stared up into the night sky; it was so peaceful, but the turmoil in her heart would not be stilled.

'Did you miss me?' A drawling voice made her heart leap, her eyes widen in shock.

'Jake . . .' She sat up, swinging her legs to the floor, and stared up into his shadowed face.

'Well, did you?' he asked, his hand reaching out to catch a tendril of her hair and twist it lightly around his finger, before curving it gently around her small ear, his finger lingering on the soft lobe and pulling gently.

He was still wearing the shorts and shirt, his hair somewhat rumpled and a day's stubble darkening his hard jaw. He looked incredibly sexy and his teasing smile promised everything. Lexi shook her head away from his hand. She was confused and angry. How did he manage to affect her like this? Every time he came near her, touched her, his masculinity hit her like a blow to the heart.

'Some half-hour,' she snapped, angry anew at his casual disregard for her feelings. She had come down earlier at his instigation only to find him gone, and gone to the lovely Lorraine. He had a damn cheek asking if she had missed him.

'You did miss me, Lexi, though getting you to admit it is probably impossible. Sorry about before, but I had an urgent call and had to leave.'

'Says you,' she scorned, knowing full well where he had been.

'At least I was only gone a couple of hours, Lexi darling.' Jake gave her a derisive smile. 'Unlike you, who vanished for years without a word.'

Lexi felt her temper flare, and getting to her feet she looked straight up into his hard face. 'And I'm sure you missed me,' she drawled scathingly, knowing very well that he had been desperate to get rid of her.

'Yes. Yes, I did.' His soft-voiced confession had Lexi's eyes flashing wide open in disbelief.

'Tell it to the marines,' she snorted inelegantly, and would have walked past him, but Jake caught her arm.

'That's your answer to everything, Lexi. Run away. I had hoped you might have matured in the last few years but it seems I was wrong, you're the same selfish child you always were.' His fingers bit into the flesh of her bare arm and she flinched at the pain. 'It doesn't matter to you who gets hurt—not your husband, your friends,

Meg and Tom.' His upper lip curled in a cynical sneer. 'Just as long as little Lexi has what she wants.'

He had some nerve calling her immature and selfish, but his mention of Meg did hit a nerve. 'I wrote to Meg,' she defended, ignoring the way her heart-beat accelerated as she stood next to Jake.

'Once, posted in Bahrain; the poor woman thought the white slavers had captured you.' One dark brow arched with sardonic amusement. 'You might fetch a good price, at that.'

His gaze roved over her in insolent appraisal. Much as she imagined a white slaver would look. Realising the idiocy of her thoughts—Jake might be a lot of things but a white slaver he was not—Lexi said, 'No,' her lips twitching with amusement. Knowing Meg, she should have realised the old woman would think of something like that. But Lexi had given the letter to a visiting Arab guest to post when he left, not wanting to reveal her whereabouts, too hurt. It was her one regret that she had not kept in touch with the old couple, but she hadn't wanted to be reminded of her old life at Forest Manor; it was too painful.

'So, you think it's amusing?' Jake's smile was chilling. 'Did it never occur to you we would worry, wonder for your safety? I was, and still am, your husband, responsible for you.'

'I'm sure you set Meg's mind at rest,' Lexi snapped and tried to jerk away from him as the full meaning of his words sank in. He had the cheek, the gall, to pretend their parting was her fault. 'You always had a way with words and women,' she said sarcastically as he pulled her violently back to him, anger flashing between them like lightning.

His dark eyes narrowed to mere slits as he looked down at her. 'God, but you're a bitch!' Rage darkened his rugged features, and Lexi gasped, her heart lurching in her breast. 'You don't care, you really don't care for anyone but yourself.'

'Isn't that the pot calling the kettle?' she spat back furiously.

'I know this,' Jake responded in a bitingly menacing voice. 'You strolled into our London apartment, agreed to our deal, and, before I could open the champagne, you were dashing out having informed me casually you were going on holiday and never wanted to see me again.' His free hand reached up and grasped a handful of her hair, pulling it loose from its slide and tangling in the red locks. 'You're a very beautiful woman, but you know how to put the knife in, Lexi; that was a master-touch, leaving the little wedding-anniversary present on the hall-table.'

'Sorry I couldn't do better,' she gritted, 'but I was short of cash at the time.' She was surprised he had even noticed the gift she had left, when he'd had his new love to occupy him.

'Oh, I got your message all right. Leave the poor sod a gift and he won't worry; after all, you were recovering from losing our child. Post-natal blues—naturally I would allow you a holiday, even though it was so hastily arranged. I called your precious Dr Bell and he was of course all in sympathy with the little wife. A holiday was the best cure; he had suggested it himself to you, and, as for your not wanting to see me, he assured me you didn't mean it—it was part of your depression, et cetera et cetera,' he drawled with icy cynicism. 'A week later, when I began looking for you, it was too late; you had vanished.'

'I'm amazed you bothered, in the circumstances,' Lexi said scathingly, while her mind absorbed the fact that Jake had looked for her. Why? She could not possibly have been wrong about what she saw and heard that day in their apartment. Could she? No. She shook her head.

'Foolishly, I was labouring under the impression that you were still depressed and might actually need me.' His strong features were harsh in the dim light. 'You thought you were clever, but not clever enough, Lexi. You will never make a fool of me or get away from me again, that I can promise.'

'That makes me quake in my shoes,' she snapped back defiantly. 'As I remember, you were never great on keeping a promise.' Thinking of his broken marriage vows, she felt an urge to hurt him as he had hurt her which compelled her to add, 'With your record I should be home free and wealthy in a few weeks.' He was a callous brute who had blackmailed her into his bed and she despised him for it. But the brush of his thigh against her, the warmth of his body ignited a trembling awareness.

Jake jerked her head back. 'You couldn't resist reminding me. But this time it will be different. I have enough money to last a hundred lifetimes, enough to satisfy even you, and, my God, I intend to make damn sure you satisfy me, Lexi,' he drawled cynically. 'And after this morning I don't think you will find our reconciliation so arduous.'

She stared at him. She had the strangest feeling she was missing something vital, but then their eyes met and fused, and her legs turned to jelly at the harsh intention she saw in his eyes. 'No.' Her neck hurt as he pulled her head further back. 'No, you can't do this to me,' she cried desperately.

'Yes,' Jake said thickly. He dragged her towards him, and she struggled, hitting out at him with her clenched fist, anywhere she could reach. 'I can do what I like with you, my less than loving wife.'

'I hate you...' His dark head descended. She tried to twist away, but his superior strength defeated her.

'Then I'd better give you reason,' he growled, his hard mouth grinding down on her, pushing her lips apart against her teeth. Her head swam, and she was sinking beneath the savage onslaught of his plundering possession. Jake's head lifted and she gasped for air.

'What the hell—Maria?' he snarled and Lexi staggered on trembling legs; she was free.

She sank down on to the lounger, breathing hard. She raised her hand to her mouth, a trembling finger tracing her swollen lips.

Jake looked down, his black brows jerking together as he saw her gesture. 'You will not wipe me out of your life as easily again, and don't you forget it,' he grated angrily, and, turning, walked towards where Maria was setting the table.

Lexi heard his brief instruction to the housekeeper. 'Hold the meal fifteen minutes, Maria.' And she watched with hurt, angry eyes as Jake strode into the house.

Dinner was a silent affair. Lexi tried to avoid looking at the man opposite her. Jake had walked back on to the terrace five minutes earlier and, with a curt instruction to Maria to serve the meal, had issued an equally curt command to Lexi.

'Sit down and eat.' He pulled out a chair for her as he did so.

Lexi did as he instructed, taking the chair he offered. He had changed into a pair of dark pleated slacks and a crisp white shirt, and looked cool and somehow remote, which suited Lexi perfectly as she had no desire to speak to him; she was still seething from their last encounter. She sipped at her glass of wine and pushed the pasta around on her plate, making little attempt to eat it.

'More wine?' Jake's cool voice broke the silence.

'No, thank you.'

His blue eyes narrowed for a second on her mutinous face. Then he topped up his glass and raising it to his mouth drained it, as much as to say she wasn't worth talking to.

Lexi shot him a look of loathing. Damn him! He was so controlled, so sure of his own diabolical power to make all obey him. Would nothing dent the overwhelming arrogance of the man? She took another sip of wine. 'Tell me, Jake, how long is your sojourn in Italy likely to last? I seem to remember you were a workaholic, not at all the type to sit around smelling the roses.'

Deliberately he forked some more pasta into his mouth and slowly chewed while his deep blue eyes, reflecting the lantern's glow in their depths, raked over her face and the hint of cleavage revealed by the open neck of her dress and then back to her face.

'A week, perhaps two.' His dark lashes lowered seductively over his gleaming eyes. 'Surely you're not in so much of a hurry to return to England that you would begrudge me my first holiday in years.' He smiled, a sinister twist of his lips, and added mockingly, 'A second honeymoon, if you like.'

'I don't like,' she spat back, and, lifting her glass to her mouth, drained the contents.

'Oh, come on, Lexi, stop this nonsense.' His voice had a sharp edge. 'We're both caught in the same trap. A savage passion we both hate but can't deny. Why lie, Lexi?' Jake demanded, an odd bitterness roughening his tone. 'You're my wife. We're here together in one of the loveliest places on earth.' He glanced around the floodlit gardens and the ocean beyond, his knowing gaze coming back to rest on Lexi. 'Forget your silly resentment and enjoy yourself.'

'Silly resentment?' She almost choked on the words. 'Is that what you call being blackmailed, having one's job, one's life taken over.'

'I'm your husband,' he said quietly with an edge of steel. 'Blackmail apart. I have the right to keep you, and, as for your job, look on it as a learning process. Now you are eminently suitable to take care of my various homes and play hostess to the cosmopolitan collection of business acquaintances I am obliged to entertain occasionally. As my social secretary and mother of my children you will have more than enough to keep you occupied.'

Various homes! And she just bet that included her old home. Social secretary? What a flaming nerve... 'Won't that be stepping on your so-faithful Lorraine's toes?' she queried derisively, hiding her pain at his mention of the word 'mother'.

'Jealous, Lexi?'

'In your dreams,' she jeered.

'Lorraine is a brilliant businesswoman, but does not suffer fools gladly; she is far too outspoken for the social niceties, and a homemaker she is not...' Jake's eyes gleamed with latent amusement. 'Whereas you are perfect for the role. Your upbringing as a diplomat's daughter has taught you how to mix with anyone. Your gift for languages, your experience looking after the wealthy clientele at the Piccolo Paradiso, all conspire to make you the ideal wife for a man in my position.'

'I wasn't aware blackmailers needed a social secretary.' She gazed at him with utter loathing. What he had said made a horrible kind of sense, and she believed him, but it hurt to finally hear the truth. Jake would carry on as he always had with the lovely Lorraine, while Lexi would be little more than a glorified housekeeper and mother of his children, wheeled out on social occasions as his polite, eminently suitable little wife.

'Enough.' Jake slapped his napkin on the table, and, reaching across, he grabbed her hand curving around the wine glass. 'Stop these foolish recriminations, Lexi. Accept you are my wife.'

'Do I have a choice?' she asked dully.

Jake regarded her with unwavering scrutiny, as if searching for something she had no knowledge of, then said with stark cynicism, 'No.'

'I didn't think so.' Bitterness laced her tone.

'Let me do the thinking for both of us. Life will be a lot easier.'

The touch of his long fingers, the intensity in his dark eyes stopped the scathing words she was about to utter. Instead, she could only gasp helplessly as he uncurled her fingers from the stem of the glass and raised her hand to his mouth, pressing a soft kiss into her palm before lacing her fingers with his own.

'Tomorrow we start our holiday.' Jake stood up, dragging her to her feet. He walked to the top of the table and she had to follow on her side. They met and his other hand grasped her shoulder. He stared down into the pale oval of her face, noting her defiant expression. 'Forget the past.'

'And enjoy a holiday?' Lexi sneered. 'I'm not that good an actress.'

'It doesn't make any difference. You don't have to act in bed,' Jake said tautly. 'I can easily seduce you, and we both know it.'

His confident assertion was true, and she hated him all the more for knowing it. 'No...' she muttered.

'Yes...' he asserted as his hand left her shoulder and gently touched her mouth, where the soft contours of her lips had swollen at the force of Jake's kiss. She shivered at his touch.

'I'm sorry if I hurt you earlier,' Jake murmured with a faintly sardonic smile, as he noted her involuntary response.

Lexi gasped as the soft pad of his thumb gently caressed her lip, sending tremors up and down her spine. She knew she should stop him, break away, but the deep husky voice, the romantic setting, all conspired against her common sense.

'You have lovely lips; let me kiss it better,' he murmured.

His thumb teased her lips and tongue. She trembled and saw no point in denying him; she couldn't. She was trapped as surely as Jake was by the physical desire that flared between them at the slightest glance. She hated it, and hated him, but she could not stop her body swaying towards him.

'I've eaten, but I'm hungry again for you,' Jake husked, and without further words he swept her up in his arms and carried her into the house...

CHAPTER EIGHT

'FOR heaven's sake, Lexi! Will you hurry up?'

She heard Jake shouting right through the house and, with one last glance at her reflection in the dressing-table mirror, she patted her loosely pinned chignon and flinging her bag over her shoulder dashed out of her room. Today they were going to Pompeii, and by the sound of it Jake was in a hurry to get started. It was his fault she was late, she thought mutinously. Instead of Maria delivering her coffee to her room this morning, it had been Jake and before she could drink it he had climbed into bed with her. Her lips were still swollen from his kisses, and the rest of her body still glowed from his loving, though it galled her to have to admit it...

She sighed as she walked down the stairs. Jake was an enigma; from the first night together in the villa when he had swept her up to bed and made passionate love to her and then got out of her bed and returned to his own, she had been trying to figure him out. But without much success. Though in all honesty she had nothing much to complain about. That was, if she discounted the fact that she had lost her job, and was being black-mailed, she told herself drily.

When she had first known Jake she had been young and naïve. Now she congratulated herself that she was mature and sophisticated enough to meet him on his own terms. There was no point in denying the sexual chemistry between them, and she knew Jake was as much a hostage to the passion that flared between them as she was herself. The hatred they felt for each other only lent their passion an added edge, a dark desire, a battle of body and wills that turned the lovemaking into a fight for control, and the bed into a battlefield with Jake always walking away victorious.

Inwardly Lexi sighed. 'Lovemaking'—that was a misnomer. Love didn't enter into their relationship. A wry smile twisted her full lips as she reached the bottom of the stairs. Lust, yes, an indefinable animal attraction; whatever label she put on it didn't really matter. At least she was mature enough to accept it as just that, without having to label it 'love'. But sometimes, in the afterglow of passion, when Jake with almost indecent haste distanced himself from her, as though to touch her in anything other than passion disgusted him, she could not help feeling, deep down in the darkest reaches of her mind, his callous rejection, and grieving the loss of the tactile, loving man she had first married.

'Lexi,' she heard the roar, and ran the short distance through the hall and out of the front door.

Jake was standing holding open the door of the lethal looking black Bugatti, a frown on his handsome face. Her heart lurched in her breast; he was wearing stylish Armani tailored shorts in a navy linen and a lighter blue polo shirt. The Mediterranean sun had darkened his skin to a deep, polished bronze, and he looked as lethal as the car.

'At last, woman. Who was it told me we had to visit Pompeii in the morning, before the sun got too hot?' he queried mockingly, then grinned wickedly.

She knew what the grin was for. 'And who was it delayed a poor girl in her bed while he had his evil way with her?' she teased back easily.

A slow, sexy smile lit his blue eyes. 'Touché. Now get in the car.'

It was like a day out of time. Jake relaxed completely from the cold, guarded man Lexi had become used to the past few days and became a typical tourist for the

day. Lexi did not question the change. Her nerves were
shot and she was glad of the respite from the constant
tension that had fizzed like an unexploded bomb between them; the least spark and they were at each other's
throats. With a sigh of contentment she settled back in
the passenger seat of the monster car and, straightening
the short skirt of her simple blue sundress over knees,
she determined to enjoy herself.

Having parked the car in the area provided, Jake surprised her by taking her hand, and, laughing together
at a middle-aged tourist buried under a mountain of
cameras, hand in hand they made their way to the entrance of the ancient city. Hundreds of tourists spilled
in an ever-increasing horde from the dozens of coaches
arriving seemingly every minute, the jostling crowd and
the multitude of different languages filling the hot
morning air.

A small, thick-set old Neapolitan man grabbed Jake's
arm. 'Guide, sir? I, Luigi, am the best.'

Jake glanced at the old man. 'I don't...'

'Yes, let's hire him,' Lexi urged. 'It is a huge place
and I hate to admit it but, although I've been once
before, I'm not that knowledgeable.'

It was a brilliant decision; Luigi, with speed and a bit
of deft manoeuvring, ushered Jake and Lexi through the
crowd, the entrance fee paid, and up to the Porta Marina,
the ancient gate that the public had to use to enter the
city, in a matter of minutes.

Jake's hand squeezed Lexi's, and she glanced ques-
tioningly up into his handsome face. 'You were right,
Luigi is worth the money solely for getting us to the front
of the queue and in.' He smiled.

'Stop.' Luigi's upraised hand and the fact that he had
planted himself directly in their path meant they could
do no other but obey, and for the next few hours the
little man managed to fill their heads with more facts

about the ancient city than any guidebook could possibly accomplish.

'First, I give you the background and then we proceed,' Luigi told them authoritatively. 'Pompeii was a settlement and first given its name in the eighth century BC. Built at the end of an ancient lava flow from what was considered the benign Mount Vesuvius, one hundred and thirty feet above sea-level at the mouth of the river Sarno, it was for centuries the trading place between the north and south Italian states, conquered by many and occupied by a few; it had a population of twenty-five thousand. Then Vesuvius, suddenly, on the twenty fourth of August, 79 AD, shortly after midday, violently erupted, blacking out the sun. Red-hot volcanic matter rained down on the hapless people, buildings crumbled and then, when the ash fell, all forms of life were extinguished. For centuries it was considered a place of evil and one thousand, six hundred years passed before excavations were begun and a further hundred and fifty years before it could be said the city was rediscovered.'

'He can certainly talk,' Jake murmured softly in Lexi's ear, 'but he knows his stuff.' And, following the little man, they strode up the steep paved ramp that led to the gate's two archways; the left hand arch had been designed for pedestrians and the other for horse-drawn carts, the ruts in the stone-paved road were deep and easily discernible, and the same gauge was still used on today's railways, Luigi informed them proudly.

'It's incredible!' Jake exclaimed, eyeing the streets and houses. 'Two thousand years on and one can see exactly how people lived.'

Lexi agreed and, walking beside him, watching the light in his eyes, the intensity with which he examined every aspect of the place, she was filled with a bittersweet memory. He had shown the same enthusiasm years ago when they had first wandered around Castle Howard.

The Temple of Venus, the mighty open space of the Forum, they wandered through them all, and gazed in awe at the remains of the Basilica dating back to pre-Roman times. The triumphal arches of the temple of Jupiter, and the Temple of Apollo caused Jake to comment, 'They certainly hedged their bets where their gods were concerned.'

'But it did no good,' Luigi piped up. 'Nature is all-powerful, always has been and always will be.'

'I think we have a homespun philosopher for a guide.' Jake bent his dark head and whispered in Lexi's ear, she glanced up at him, a smile curving her full lips.

'I think you may be right,' she murmured as Luigi led them into the Forum Baths.

'See: hot and cold baths; central heating; drainage; everything you would find in a modern city today. They had everything we have today. Nothing changes,' Luigi declared, and as they walked on he pointed out what had once been a dress shop, and two doors down a barber's shop.

Grinning at Jake, Luigi said, 'Then as now, the lady went to the boutique, and the man visited the barber and waited to pick up his lady and pay the bill. Nothing changes.' Jake and Luigi chuckled in masculine bonding, while Lexi gritted her teeth and grinned, thinking, Male chauvinists.

Further on they stared in awe at the brilliantly coloured wall-paintings in the Villa of the Mysteries. Outside again, they gazed sombrely through iron bars into a warehouse where dozens of common household items, bowls and jugs and figures, an arm, a torso lay, all coated in the pale grey stone.

In a glass case lay the body of a young woman, obviously pregnant, petrified in stone for all eternity. Lexi shivered and, freeing her hand from Jake's, walked away. She looked around at the high walls, the scrolled pillars, the streets and houses, her eyes misting with tears.

She felt an arm curve around her shoulder, strong fingers kneading the soft flesh. 'Are you OK, Lexi? The heat getting to you?' Jake's deep voice asked quietly. She glanced up through thick lashes, and noted the concern in his dark eyes.

'Yes, no. I don't know,' she murmured.

'Reminded you, did it? The pregnant woman.'

Her eyes widened. Could this be Jake, the ruthless entrepreneur? Since when had he become so sensitive? 'Yes, a little perhaps. I miscarried, but that woman lost everything, and it suddenly struck me, even with all these people around——' she gestured with a wave of her hand at the dozens of tourists as they strolled along '—there is something about this place, an aura of sadness, doom.' She unconsciously shook her head to dispel the feeling of melancholy.

'I wasn't much help when you lost the baby, was I, Lexi?'

His words stopped her in her tracks, and she could think of nothing to say. The pressure of his hand on her shoulder turned her around to face him. With his free hand he lifted her chin. 'I'm truly sorry, Lexi. I let you down, the very moment you needed me most.'

The sincerity in his tone, the deep regret in his indigo eyes convinced Lexi he was telling the truth as he saw it. 'Oh. I wouldn't say that.' She lowered her lashes, suddenly confused by Jake's confession. 'I was depressed, not really aware of anything very much.' If she had been more alert to her surroundings she might have realised sooner that he was having an affair with Lorraine, the thought hit her. And, shrugging his hand off her shoulder, she added, 'I'm sure you did your best,' and moved on.

'No, damn it!' Jake caught her arm. 'No, I didn't. I was so caught up in my business troubles, I didn't give you as much attention as you deserved.'

Lexi glanced up at him. Business troubles. Looking back, she realised he had hinted as much at the time, but she had been too wrapped in her own grief to take much notice. Was he telling the truth? She studied his handsome face; his expression was stern but serious, and she was stunned by the depths of emotion she glimpsed fleetingly in his dark eyes.

'I couldn't talk about the loss of our son, it was too painful. But I want you to know, Lexi. Whatever our differences, when and if we have another child, I will be there for you every step of the way.'

A lump formed in her throat and she blinked hard to vanquish the threatening tears. 'Thank you for that,' she said softly. She believed him, all of it. So where did that leave her? she wondered. Could it be that Jake had turned to Lorraine simply for sex, when she herself had lost interest in it? It would explain why he hadn't married Lorraine. But did it make his betrayal any less if that was the case? She didn't know . . . and, catching the side of Jake's shirt, she added, 'Come on. Poor Luigi is going to lose us if we don't hurry up.' She urged him forward.

'You OK?' Jake asked, slipping his arm around her shoulder, a rather wry smile twitching the corners of his hard mouth at her blunt changing of the subject.

'Of course.' Lexi smiled back. But his confession had jolted her more than she cared to admit.

Striding along after the tireless Luigi, they walked along streets with pavements and gutters, a bar with a classic painting on the wall of a group of men cheating at a game of cards with the aid of a mirror.

'See, nothing changes.' Luigi laughed, indicating the painting, but Lexi was barely listening.

For the past few days she had lived in a sexual daze. But Jake's words had reminded her exactly what she was committed to. He had said she owed him a child, but she had conveniently blocked the message from her mind. She had nursed a hazy idea: a few months of Jake and

sex, till his desire for her was burnt out, and then
freedom. Suddenly it wasn't so simple. What if she got
pregnant and had his child? She knew after losing one
child that if she was lucky enough to get a second chance
she would never be able to walk away from her own
baby. She cast a sidelong glance at Jake. His interest was
captured by the lead piping at the side of yet another
villa, and for a moment she studied his rugged features.
Jake was not the sort of man to let her walk away with
a child. What he owned, he kept. She shivered at the
thought of a lifetime with Jake without love, never
knowing if she could trust him. Worse: how would a
child feel, brought up in that kind of atmosphere?

'Cold?' Jake's demand and husky laugh broke into
her chaotic thoughts.

'No, no,' she reiterated and, pointing to the lead pipe,
she said the first thing that came into her head, 'I
suppose, with your being in construction, this is doubly
interesting to you.'

He glanced down at her, his blue eyes narrowing, his
dark face suddenly guarded. 'Not really, my business is
much more diversified now. I have little to do with construction. After the collapse of the property market a
few years back I concentrated my efforts on finance.'

'Finance...' But the Jake she remembered had been
a builder, a self-made man, and mad keen on his
Docklands development. He had told her once he had
taken a business and finance course at night-school, but
she thought he would have stuck with construction.

'Yes, with the help of our mutual friend Carl
Bradshaw and his German connections, I made a killing
in Deutchmarks, when the pound fell out of the ERM
and was devalued. It's amazing how easy it is to make
money when you have a beautiful mercenary woman as
an incentive,' he drawled mockingly.

Lexi wished she had kept her mouth shut; his crack
was aimed at her. At least she thought it was, and in a

rush of honesty she told him, 'I never wanted your money, Jake; in fact I've never looked at the account you opened for me, not since I left England.'

'Do you know, I almost believe you.' Jake hugged her and pushed her in front of him. 'Come on, the guide is escaping.'

Inexplicably Lexi's heart felt lighter as Luigi led them into the House of Vetii, a villa restored almost completely intact, and perhaps the most notorious in Pompeii, known for its pornographic paintings and statue. Within minutes Lexi could see why as she followed behind Luigi. Lexi stopped and turned bright scarlet at the statue in front of her. She heard Jake's chuckle behind her, but didn't dare turn around as Luigi burst into speech.

'The poor man suffered from an uncommon disease, as you can see.' And Lexi could see all too clearly the exaggerated masculinity of the man. 'A state of permanent readiness, shall I say.' His old face split with a huge grin. 'Many male tourists ask me how to contract this disease.' And with an arch of his bushy eyebrows, and an open palmed salute he added, 'But unfortunately, I cannot say.' And cackled with laughter at his own joke.

Lexi felt Jake's arms curve around her waist to hold her firmly against him, the back of her legs through the fine fabric of her sundress brushing against his thighs; she could feel the warmth of his breath at her throat.

'I can,' Jake whispered teasingly in her ear. 'All a man has to do is stay around you, Lexi, darling. You keep me in that state permanently.'

Herself and how many other women? she wondered, a flash of pain—or was it jealousy—piercing her breast. 'Jake,' she admonished. She could feel the stirring of his masculine interest all too plainly against her. 'There are people around,' she hissed in embarrassment.

'Shame.' Jake gave an exaggerated sigh and Lexi, pulling free, dashed after Luigi.

For the rest of the tour through the house, Lexi hardly noticed the magnificent wall paintings or the lovely garden; she was too intensely aware of Jake. He had caught up with her and rested one arm possessively over her shoulders, his long stride slowed to match hers, the brush of his thigh against her leg, the warmth of his hard body, the musky male scent of him all conspired to make her pulse-rate rocket. She tried to tell herself it was all the walking, the stifling heat of the noonday sun, but she knew she was only fooling herself.

'You're very quiet,' Jake said softly as they walked once more down yet another paved street. 'Had enough for one day?'

'It is rather hot, and the crowds...' She trailed off as Luigi stopped once more, but she was flattered at Jake's evident concern.

'We now go to the great Amphitheatre; today we still build a sports stadium in much the same design. Nothing changes. The only new inventions since the wheel are the new power sources, new ways to kill each other——'

'Very true, Luigi,' Jake interrupted the old man. 'But my wife has had enough for one day—the heat.'

'I see, I see. It is lunch time.' Luigi smiled, his dark eyes sliding over Jake with his protective arm around Lexi. 'Also, I think you enjoy a siesta, no?' His black eyes sought Jake's and he started to laugh. 'As I say, nothing changes. You marry, you make love, you make babies.' Jake's responsive chuckle mingled with the older man's laughter as Luigi led them speedily to the exit.

Lexi looked at Luigi, and then sideways at Jake. His eyes were crinkled at the corners in amusement, his firm mouth relaxed in a singularly masculine grin; he looked carefree, happy and vitally male.

'A siesta sounds good to me, sweetheart,' Jake drawled turning his glittering blue eyes down to capture hers.

It was at that moment it hit her like a thunderbolt. She loved Jake. Luigi was right, 'you marry, you make love, you make babies', and she realised, staring at Jake, that that was exactly what she wanted, had probably always been what she wanted with this man. She blinked and tore her gaze away from his handsome face, unable to answer the sensual message in Jake's eyes, too afraid she would give herself away completely. 'Whatever you say,' she murmured, and didn't see the flash of anger darken his bright eyes at her dull response.

In the car, Lexi laid her head back against the head-rest and closed her eyes. Jake had paid Luigi hand-somely and promised they would return, and she had smilingly accepted the old man's congratulations on having such a handsome and generous husband. But now, in the close confines of the car with Jake's strong body only inches from her own, his attractive face set in a look of determined concentration as he urged the car along the treacherous winding coast-road, avoiding the wild antics of most of the Italian drivers, she was left to her own thoughts, and they were anything but pleasant.

She could not believe her own stupidity. When Jake had blackmailed his way back into her life, she had told herself she hated him, and burnt with resentment at the ease with which he could tumble her into his bed. But at the same time she congratulated herself on being more than a match for him. She was quite capable of meeting him on the same sophisticated sexual level as the rest of his friends, Lorraine in particular. Now she recognised the depths of her own self-deception.

Married or not, five years' celibacy should have told her something. She was not the type to sleep with a man without love—not that Jake *slept* with her, the hurtful thought flashed in her mind; he made a point of leaving

her bed and returning to his own... She had pretended
to herself she didn't care, when in reality she cared far
too much. She had loved him as a teenager and she still
did. For years she had deceived herself into believing she
hated him when in fact it had simply been the only way
she could get through life without him, a way of masking
the deep pain his betrayal had caused her.

'Do you want to stop for lunch?' Jake's voice interrupted her reverie, her eyes flashed open and she looked
at Jake, then just as quickly away again.

'No, thank you. I'm not hungry,' she said flatly. She
just wanted to get back to the villa and lock herself in
her bedroom. The thought of sitting in a restaurant
making polite conversation with Jake was an added strain
she could do without. It was bad enough realising she
still loved him. She needed to be on her own for a while,
time to sort out her emotions, decide where she went
from here.

A growing sense of despair settled in her heart as, with
a grinding of gears, the car speeded up. After Jake's
revelation about the baby they had lost, they had seemed
to reach a new understanding this morning. But now,
with the fear of revealing her love for him uppermost
in her mind, they had slid back into the familiar tension-
packed atmosphere of the past few days. Lexi didn't
know what she could do about it.

Without speaking they drove through Sorrento and
along Amalfi Drive. She chanced a swift sidelong glance
at Jake. He was frowning, his dark eyes narrowed against
the sun, his mouth a grim straight line; her laughing
companion of the morning had changed into a darkly
brooding, dangerous man.

She looked down at her clasped hands folded neatly
in her lap, and was lost again in her own painful
thoughts. Jake wanted her but he didn't love her. How
could she live the rest of her life with a man who did

not love her and whom she did not trust? It was
hopeless...

Jake, bringing the car to a screeching halt outside the
front door of the villa, made her sit up and take notice.
But, before Lexi had managed to unfasten her safety-
belt, Jake was out of the car and had the passenger door
open and was reaching in to help her; his hand closed
firmly over her upper arm and he almost dragged her
from the car.

'Move it,' he snapped and his voice sounded rough.
He led her into the house and up the wide staircase, his
anger a tangible force in the still air.

'Where's the fire?' she tried to joke but, as her eyes
clashed with his, she had her answer—it was in the
glistening depths of Jake's eyes. Her pulse raced, a
sudden heat igniting in her lower stomach.

'You know...' One dark brow arched cynically as he
pushed her before him into his bedroom, his fingers
gripping the flesh of her arm. He shut the door behind
him and leant back against it, roughly pulling her into
the hard heat of his long body.

'Luigi was right, nothing changes,' he rasped sav-
agely, and she caught her breath as his lips moved against
hers. 'You're running away from me again, and I won't
tolerate it.'

Lexi, running away! With his long arms like bands of
steel around her waist, she knew she had to be hearing
things. She leant back and raised puzzled eyes to his,
taking in the hard planes of his ruggedly chiselled features. 'Unless I'm dreaming, I am very much here.' She
quipped, trying to sound casual, to defuse the tension
cracking around them.

'Physically, yes. But mentally you ran away ages ago,
as we left Pompeii.' His eyes narrowed fractionally, and
she sensed the anger lying beneath the surface of his
control. 'You did it in London, listened and agreed with
me, and then vanished. Those innocent eyes haze with

purple and it's as if a curtain has drawn across your mind, shutting out anything and anyone.' His warm breath fanned her temple. 'I'm damned if I'm going to let you get away with it again.'

'Why?' she said simply. 'You told me days ago it was my body alone that interested you.'

'I've changed my mind; it's not solely a woman's prerogative.' Jake taunted and his hands pulled her close so that she was made all too conscious of his arousal. 'I want to know your every thought.'

'Taking me in anger is hardly likely to make me bare my soul to you——' Lexi drew an unsteady breath '—even if I wanted to.' And she did want to; she ached to tell him she loved him, let go of her emotions completely, but she dared not. He had hurt her too much in the past. Suddenly the thought sneaked into her head: surely it was a step in the right direction if Jake actually did want to know her better, deepen the relationship. She loved him, and if their marriage was to have any chance at all it was up to her to try and make it work, to try and win Jake's love. That was always supposing he was capable of such an emotion, she thought wryly.

'I sometimes doubt you have a soul,' Jake snarled. 'The only way to reach you is this,' he muttered with menacing softness against her lips, just before his mouth ground down on hers.

She sighed, her breath mingling with his. Their tongues touched, danced, writhed, and she felt herself falling, down, down, down once more into the depths of desire, a passionate flood of need only Jake could arouse.

Suddenly he moved, thrusting her away from him. 'Get undressed, Lexi,' he said deliberately, swiftly pulling his shirt over his head, his hands going to the fastening of his shorts. 'Come on...!' A hard dark gleam sprang alive in his eyes. 'I'm in no mood for patience...'

She stood transfixed, her eyes roaming over his naked chest, the dark whorls of body hair glistening in the hot afternoon sun. A strange languor hung in the air and, as if in a dream, Lexi did as he said, whisking her simple sundress over her head, but all the time she watched as he slid his bermudas down his thighs along with his briefs. Even when he stepped towards her, his fingers digging into the skin of her shoulders as he pulled her close, she could not tear her gaze away from his strongly muscled, virile frame. She knew she should be afraid, there was a menacing calculation about his movements, but oddly she wasn't. She loved him, and she wanted him...

Lexi sucked in her breath and raised her eyes to his, and when she met his darkly unyielding expression she trembled, but something gave her the courage to try and deflect his anger.

'Why hurry, Jake?' she asked flirtatiously. Lowering her long lashes half over her eyes, she reached out a finger and trailed it lightly down the hard column of his throat. 'We can take Luigi's advice, and have a siesta,' she declared huskily.

She had surprised him. His forbidding expression lightened perceptibly, his sensuous mouth tilted at the corners in the beginnings of a smile. 'Damn you, Lexi...you confuse me to hell.' A masculine chuckle escaped him, his anger waning. 'But I wouldn't have it any other way.' And, swinging her in his arms, he carried her to the bed, his body following her down; he shifted his weight until he was lying heavily across her chest, crushing the soft roundness of her breasts against his chest.

His mouth came down on hers in a hard, hot kiss. His hands slid down her body, along her thighs, pushing her legs apart. He kissed her again, a ruthless demand that contained the lingering traces of anger and masculine frustration. She felt a shiver of fear ripple down her spine, but somehow she knew he would not hurt her, and she opened her mouth to welcome him, surprising him yet again. He reared back, a question in his navy blue eyes.

Lexi smiled and deliberately lifted her small hand and stroked the firm skin of his stomach, and lower, entranced by the lightning response of his aroused body. Jake moved over her, his tongue driving into her mouth, and she had the feeling she was being seduced, physically dominated, as if he needed to show her he was in control.

'You want me, you can't help yourself. Whatever else you are, Lexi, in this you are mine and mine alone,' he husked, and lowered his head to suck on the rosy tips of her breasts, bringing them to throbbing peaks of desire; his fingers slid down between her parted thighs, and began moving in quick sensuous patterns that had Lexi trembling all over.

Lexi's eyes widened to their fullest extent, her body arched, the breath nearly crushed from her, but she was ready for him as Jake drove into her soft, moist centre with a fierce aggression that made her shudder on the pinnacle of delight. For a timeless space he did not move, making her aware of the full weight of his possession, while withholding the release she craved. She cried his name. The sound of his name on her lips shattered Jake's control. Their bodies, bathed in perspiration, slid together, rocking, moving in a shimmering white-hot culmination so closely entwined they spun as one into the fiery rapture of climax.

Ages later Lexi groaned, but still she clung to Jake, reluctant to move, if not incapable of movement, she thought fuzzily. Finally, she lifted heavy lashes to find Jake staring down at her. She smiled lovingly, her soft gaze roaming over his darkly flushed face.

Jake rolled on to his side, one large hand supporting his head; a smile curved his lips and sparkled in his eyes. His other hand deliberately stroked across her full breasts. 'I could easily get addicted to this siesta idea,' he offered lazily, rubbing his mouth lightly against hers. 'But right now, I need lunch.'

It was hardly the words of love she had been dreaming about, but it was a step in the right direction, she thought with hope in her heart.

CHAPTER NINE

LEXI, wearing a brief black bikini with a floaty black and pink silk patterned overblouse on top, and carrying a matching beach bag, the whole ensemble a present from Jake, strolled out on to the terrace and down the steps to the swimming-pool. Shrugging out of her shirt, she flopped listlessly on to a convenient sun-lounger, rummaged in her bag and found her sunglasses and pushed them on her nose. Sweeping her long hair round to one side of her neck, she lay back down on the lounger and tried to relax.

The heat was almost unbearable, in the nineties; she glanced around the colourful sweet-scented garden, the pool, and the view of the sea beyond. She had watched Jake leave after a shared informal lunch in the comfort of the air-conditioned kitchen. He had said he had business to attend to... Maybe he had... right at this moment she didn't give a damn!

Tomorrow it would be exactly two weeks since she had moved into the villa. This morning, as she had been idly looking through her diary, ruefully reflecting on the fact it had been chock-full of appointments up until Jake had stormed back into her life and cost her her job, it had suddenly hit her. She was a week overdue with her period. She tried telling herself it wasn't important. What was a week, for heaven's sake? But, for a girl who had never been so much as a day late except the one time she had been pregnant, the week was beginning to assume gigantic proportions.

Instinctively her hand stroked across her flat stomach, her feelings ambivalent. She had always longed for a child after her tragic miscarriage, she freely admitted, but in the circumstances...

Restless, she jumped to her feet and dropping her glasses on the lounger she took a running dive head-first into the pool. The shock of the cool water was a balm to her overheated flesh. She swam a few quick lengths and then turned over on to her back and floated, her mind idly wandering over the past.

Yesterday Jake had taken her in his power-boat to Capri. They had strolled around the town and Jake had ushered her into a myriad designer boutiques, and insisted on buying her a host of clothes: the bikini she was wearing now, and an extravagant evening gown he told her she had to have for a special engagement tonight. Another of his secrets!

Sexually they were compatible, the chemistry between them explosive. Jake made love to her every day—sometimes he came to her bed at night, sometimes by this very pool. He just had to look at her a certain way, a touch of his hand; their passion for each other was insatiable.

Ever since their trip to Pompeii, when Jake had talked about the loss of their child, they seemed to have developed a kind of rapport. They had long, interesting, sometimes argumentative conversations about music, art, the state of Italian politics, which was a subject one could debate a lifetime without running out of steam, Lexi thought with a grin. She could almost convince herself that her plan to win his love was succeeding, except for the fact that they still never woke up in the morning sharing the same bed. Lexi had not the nerve to ask why. She wasn't sure she would like the answer.

Jake never shared his thoughts, his inner self, as he had when they were first married. Though, her own innate honesty forced her to admit, she was just as guilty in that respect. Her pride and fear of being hurt contrived to prevent her revealing her own feelings.

Things could be worse, Lexi conceded, though he had infuriated her about her car. Jake had arranged for it to be delivered back to the hotel, saying there was no way he would allow her to drive the 'old wreck' and, in any case, strictly speaking it belonged to the hotel. He might as well have said she could not go out without him, because that was what it boiled down to. But, to give Jake his due, he had taken her out every day. To Sorrento, Naples and some of the smaller islands, and they had had fun. Jake was a good companion when he wanted to be, she mused. But one major problem was the same as always—Lorraine. The woman was forever calling Jake, and he dashed off at the summons. Lexi knew it was business, and she didn't really think Jake was still having an affair with Lorraine, mainly because she doubted that even Jake had that much stamina, given how often he and Lexi made love. But a nagging suspicion about the relationship haunted Lexi. There was something...

'Aghhh...' she screamed, a second before her head slid under the water. A hand had caught her ankle, pulling her deeper and deeper beneath the water, and then a strong arm wrapped around her and she was shooting back to the surface. Choking and spluttering, trying to sweep her tangled mass of hair from her face and at the same time dry her eyes, she screeched, 'What the hell did you do that for?' And tossing back her head, she looked up into the wickedly laughing face of Jake.

Clasping her around the middle, he hauled her between his muscular thighs. His lips brushed hers and, grinning, he said, 'Sour grapes... You looked so relaxed floating around, while I've spent the last few hours hot and harassed driving into Naples. When I got back and saw you from the window I couldn't resist the temptation.'

'Pig,' she retaliated, whacking her hand through the water and splashing him in the face. He jumped back, his legs releasing her, and Lexi chuckled at his astonished expression.

'You wanna fight rough, babe?' Jake drawled in a mock American accent, before placing his hands on her shoulders and dunking her again.

Lexi stayed under the water and swam between his long legs. Surfacing behind him, she flung her arms around his neck and tried to pull him over backwards. But his superior strength showed as he put his hands behind him under her stomach and flipped her high in the air and she found herself swung up and over his head in a somersault to land flat on her back in the water.

'Had enough?' Jake taunted, hauling her up by the front clasp of her bikini top.

Treading water, she yelled, 'You beast!' It was all right for Jake, he was so much taller that he could stand on the bottom with no trouble, she fumed, and tried to splash him again. Their laughter echoed on the summer air, until Lexi let out a yelp as she realised Jake was waving the top of her bikini around his head. She folded her arms across her chest. 'Pervert, give me it back.'

'One down, one to go.' Jake let out a war cry and dived on top of Lexi. In a tangle of arms and legs they sank to the bottom of the pool.

When Lexi surfaced again, she was folded once more in Jake's strong thighs, one of his hands supported her back so she was almost lying on top of the water and in his other hand he was proudly holding aloft both parts of her bikini.

'To the winner, the spoils,' he crowed triumphantly.

Lexi's gaze slid over his broad shoulders up the strong line of his throat to his proud head; his hair was plastered to his skull and he looked like a young boy again. Her heart squeezed in her breast, she loved him so. He must have seen something of what she was feeling in her eyes because he said her name.

'Lexi.' Jake pulled her up, his dark head bent, blocking out the sun, all laughter gone, as his mouth brushed hers.

Naked in his arms, the water lapping softly around them, Lexi curved her slender arms around his neck, and, her lips parting, she kissed him back.

He groaned, his hands catching her legs and wrapping them around his waist, as his tongue darted into her mouth in quick, searching thrusts.

Lexi crossed her feet behind him and clung. His hands stroked round her waist and up to palm her breasts. She felt the force of his masculine aggression urgent between her thighs, only the flimsy fabric of his Spandex briefs and the tantalising brush of the water preventing his completing the act they both craved.

'Jake, we can't,' she whimpered as his teeth nipped the rigid peak of one breast.

'Lexi, we can.' He trailed the words up her breast and over her throat, to find her mouth. 'Trust me.'

'We'll drown,' she moaned.

'Only in each other.'

Lexi felt his hands under her thighs at the edge of his swimming-trunks, pushing them down. She gasped, and tightened her grip on his shoulders as he reared up and into her in one swift movement, his hands gripping her waist, he held her impaled by his masculine strength.

She had never felt anything so erotic in her life; the water gave a weightlessness to her limbs and the contrast of the cool water and the hot sun on her naked flesh, the driving force of Jake, her breasts buried in the soft, wet hair of his muscular chest, the muffled groans, the heady scent of flowers and sea air all combined to make it a tapestry of scent, sound, sight and sensational eroticism, culminating in a shuddering ecstasy.

'We didn't drown,' she whimpered, still clinging to Jake's neck as he half-swam and half-walked to the side of the pool and, lifting her up, he sat her on the edge, and then hauled himself up and proceeded to collapse flat on his back, his feet still dangling in the water.

'I promised myself we would try that before we have to leave,' Jake rasped breathlessly, and getting to his feet he added, 'It was even better than my fantasy.'

But Lexi had heard. She sat up, only then remembering she was naked, she bent her knees and clasped her hands defensively around them. 'Leave? When are you leaving?' she asked quietly.

Glancing up, her eyes lingered helplessly. Jake, with water still trickling down his glorious golden body, was beautifully made. Thick black hair shadowed down his bronzed body to a flat stomach, powerful long legs, and a blatant masculinity that made her shiver with remembered delight. She looked up into his eyes and was stunned by the flash of pain she thought she saw in their shadowed depths.

'*We*——' he accentuated the single word '—are leaving on Monday. I have to be in London for a meeting in the afternoon.' He glanced at the waterproof Rolex on his wrist. 'But for the moment I suggest you go and gild the lily; we have to go out in an hour.'

'Just like that, no discussion?' Lexi prompted. Rising to her feet, she walked to the lounger and picked up her shirt and slipped it on. Jake might be happy with his nudity, but she, stupidly maybe, found it difficult to behave naturally stark naked—a relic of her convent upbringing...

Jake watched her with cool, assessing eyes and, when she turned back to face him, his hand reached out and long fingers tipped up her chin. 'There's nothing to discuss; you're my wife, you go where I go. Don't try to make a battle out of it, Lexi.'

'I wasn't,' she told him steadily. 'But I would like to be kept informed. It is my life you're playing with,' she couldn't help sniping sarcastically. While in her heart she wondered how they could make love one minute and end up facing up like two strangers the next.

As if sensing her dilemma, Jake's hand slipped from her chin to her shoulder, his fingers squeezing her tender flesh. 'You worry too much.' His dark head bent and his lips brushed along her brow, rather like a father reassuring a child. 'And be assured, I'm not playing. I've never been more serious in my life. But we'll talk later, after the party.'

'Party?'

'Damn, it's supposed to be a secret. Your half-naked body never fails to scramble my brain,' he offered with a chuckle. 'Now, run along while I have a swim, there's a good girl.' And spinning her around he slapped a helping hand on her bottom. 'Later, we'll talk.'

Lexi fumed at his pat and chauvinistic attitude, and, without thinking, she spun back around and, catching Jake completely off guard, she planted both hands on his broad chest, stuck her foot behind him and pushed. He hit the water with a very satisfactory splash, and Lexi, arching one elegant eyebrow, stood smiling down at the spluttering, enraged male and drawled sarcastically, 'Have a nice swim, there's a good boy.' And, grinning, she ran back to the house.

Later, washed and dressed in the designer gown Jake had given her, a strapless creation with a deep jade-green bodice that lovingly traced the swell of her full breasts, nipped into her slender waist and fell to mid-calf in shimmering handkerchief layers of multi-shaded green chiffon, she walked into the salon, and she was not feeling quite so brave.

She stopped inside the door. Jake was leaning against the mantelshelf, his dark head bent over whatever it was he was turning over in his hand, and he looked dropdead gorgeous... There was no other way to describe him. His evening-jacket was cream and with it he wore a white silk dress-shirt and a rich blue bow-tie; the jacket was hanging open to reveal a matching blue cummerbund, and his other hand, in the pocket of his pants, pulled the fabric taut across his muscular thigh. She couldn't seem to drag her eyes away. Jake had always been a conservative dresser, but tonight he looked slightly flamboyant and all virile, powerful male.

Lexi swallowed with difficulty. 'I'm ready,' she managed to say steadily, and watched as Jake lifted his head from his contemplation of whatever he had in his hand.

His deep blue eyes blazed as he made no effort to hide his masculine appreciation, his gaze travelling with slow, sensual scrutiny from her mass of red hair clipped behind her small ears with matching pearl-studded combs, falling in a mass of curls over her shoulders, to her lovely, if rather wary face. She did not need much make-up, her softly tanned skin glowed with health, but she had paid special attention to her eyes, outlining their shape with a brown eyeliner, and a soft dusting of muted taupe shadow on her lids, finished off with a brown-black mascara to emphasise her long lashes.

Lexi had no idea how stunning and slightly exotic she looked, and Jake's continued silent survey was beginning to get to her. 'I said——'

'I heard.' Jake cut in, his brilliant eyes lifting from the soft curve of her breasts to her face. 'You really have grown up into the most seductive-looking woman it has ever been my pleasure to see,' he drawled softly and, straightening, laughed, a low, husky sound, as Lexi felt herself blush from head to toe.

'Surely you can't still be shy?' Jake grated softly, crossing the room in a few lithe strides. 'Though I must admit blushing becomes you.' And he reached out and caught her small hand in his.

The contact sent a shock of electrifying awareness through her slim body. She had only to look at him to recall the hard power of his male body in hers, the wet satin skin beneath her seeking fingers. She raised her eyes to his; his hair was still damp and fell in a slight wave across his broad forehead. Her face burnt, her pulse quickened. It wasn't fair that only one man should be so fatally attractive to her, when she knew, sadly, there must have been dozens of women in Jake's life over the past few years. The thought rapidly cooled her fluttering emotions.

'I want you to have this.' Jake's voice quivered along her nerves, and she looked down to where her hand lay in his in time to see him slip a diamond-encrusted gold ring on to her wedding finger.

'What? Why?' she stammered, staring in amazement at the glittering jewel, alongside the plain gold band. It must have cost a fortune.

'Because it's necessary for the wife of a man in my position.' His dark eyes sought and held hers, something unfathomable in the indigo depths. 'And, as I quickly discovered, a simple gold band was never really your style, was it?'

Lexi stared back at him, speechless; he could hurt her so easily with one unkind slur.

'Well! Do you like it, Lexi darling?' he demanded hardly.

She masked the flicker of pain in her violet eyes by quickly lifting her hand and admiring the diamond ring. 'It's lovely. Thank you,' she said politely, thinking that if Jake had truly loved her a ring-pull from a beer can would have done.

'So gracious, so polite. Oh, hell!' Jake suddenly swept her into his arms, his mouth covering hers; she expected an angry ravishment, instead his lips moved over hers in an achingly tender kiss. 'Sorry, Lexi, I swore tonight I would keep my cynical barbs to myself. Tonight is yours.'

Lexi gazed into his serious face, her violet eyes wide and puzzled. Jake lifted her hand and kissed the glittering ring on her finger.

'Forget what I said before. I bought you the ring because I wanted you to have it. Five years ago, it wasn't your fault.' He grimaced wryly. 'You were so young and I swept you into marriage without giving you time to think. I didn't think much myself at the time. I was thirty, a lot older and should have known better, but I wanted you. I saw you, took you, and I never even bought you an engagement ring. Then to cap it all I broke my promise to you.'

'It doesn't matter,' Lexi murmured. He had finally admitted he was to blame for their separation, and somehow it gave her no joy.

'But it does. Do you realise these past two weeks are the nearest I have had to a holiday in my whole life? You were right...'

Startled, Lexi waited, sure she was about to hear something of vital importance to their relationship, but at that moment the doorbell rang, and the moment was gone...

'Damn, the limousine is here. We'll continue this later, Lexi,' Jake said softly and taking her arm ushered her out of the house to the waiting car.

'Why the chauffeur?' she asked as she settled in the back seat of the huge car and Jake slid in beside her.

'Because tonight, my sweet, we are celebrating, and I intend to drink champagne with my very lovely wife, and I don't fancy risking the Amalfi Drive after downing a few.'

The party was a total and utter surprise to Lexi, but a delightful one. Jake led her into the foyer of the Piccolo Paradiso, saying he had some papers to collect from Lorraine, and did she want to have a word with Anna on Reception while she waited for him? Lexi hid her dismay at the mention of the other woman and, totally unsuspecting, she crossed the marble foyer towards the reception desk, idly noticing the dining-room doors were closed, which was unusual. Still, it wasn't her problem any more, she thought with a tinge of regret.

Then suddenly the doors were flung open and a crowd of laughing, smiling faces swept into the foyer, all shouting, '*Augurio*!' Lexi felt Jake's familiar arm curve around her waist as she was swept into the dining-room. Moisture hazed her lovely eyes as she saw the banner over the small band-stand. 'Good Luck, Long Life and Happiness, Lexi.'

She was swamped with well-wishers. The whole staff of the hotel appeared to be present along with the guests; it made a huge glittering, laughing crowd. The champagne flowed like water and to her amazement she spotted Signor Monicelli.

'Is Marco all right?' she asked after hugging the old man.

'Doing very well, thanks to your good husband,' Signor Monicelli replied, adding, 'Marriage suits you, Lexi, you look radiant.'

Anna grabbed her arm and demanded to know if there were any more back in England like Jake. Franco, all the housemaids, the porters, even the kitchen staff insisted on congratulating her, and all the time Jake kept at her side.

Someone shoved a glass of champagne in her hand, and before she knew it she was up on the stage being presented with an exquisite bronze sculpture of a sea nymph. Signor Monicelli made a brilliant and flattering speech, extolling Lexi's virtues, until she was scarlet with embarrassment.

Lexi held the beautiful bronze in one hand and stroked it gently with the other... A lump formed in her throat and she could hardly speak, one tear escaped from her hazed eyes. She swallowed hard, and then Jake's hand clasped her waist, giving her his support, and she

managed to make a rather tearful but heartfelt speech
of thanks. 'Thank you all, and I will never forget you.'

Jake led her from the stage and she glanced up at him,
a question in her lovely eyes. 'You did this for me, Jake?'

'Your friends insisted,' he said, non-committal.

'But what about the hotel guests.' Most she recognised as regular visitors, but a few were strangers to her.

'I simply told them the hotel dining-room was closed
for the night, but they were welcome to join the party.'

'It must have cost you a fortune,' she murmured—the
champagne was vintage, she noted, and dinner was a
superb buffet, with lobster and caviar, the long table
groaning with the weight of the food.

'You deserve it, Lexi, love.' His dark head bent, his
mouth erotically nibbling her small ear. 'You're worth
a thousand times more to me than a party, and later I
intend to prove it to you once and for all. We have to
put the past behind us, forgive and forget. No more secrets, no more separate beds. Trust me.'

Hope burst in her heart at Jake's muffled words, and,
glancing sideways up at him through thick lashes, she
was stunned to see a tender, caring light in his deep blue
eyes. 'Jake...' She put her hand on his chest. Was it
possible? Could they start afresh? Yes, her heart sang.
She could forgive him everything if he loved her.

'Later.'

'Alexandra.' A deep voice rang out, silencing the
crowd.

Lexi turned and gasped her pleasure at the man ac-
costing her. 'Ali!' she exclaimed. He was dressed in the
flowing white robes of the desert, and flanked on either
side by two bodyguards. Sheik Ali al Kahim was an old
friend from her childhood days when her father was
consulate in his small middle Eastern country; they had
played together as children and coincidentally met up
again at the Piccolo Paradiso where Ali was an honoured
guest once a year, but usually in the spring. 'What are

you doing here?' she demanded as he swept her up in a
bear hug then put her back on her feet.

'My yacht is in the port for a few hours. I rang the
hotel to speak with you and heard you are married and
leaving. How could you do this to me, little Alexandra?
And who is the lucky man?'

Jake, with his arm reaching out to pull Lexi into his
side, said curtly, 'I am.'

Lexi effected the introduction, her worried gaze
swinging between the two men. Jake was attractive, but
Ali, the same age as herself, was strikingly beautiful, as
tall as Jake with huge brown eyes and the classic features of a Greek god. Jake took one look at him and
seemed furious.

'You have my congratulations, Mr Taylor. You are a
very fortunate man. But I have only myself to blame I
delayed too long.'

Delayed what too long? Lexi wondered, and then was
stunned as Ali presented her with a long velvet box.

'A wedding gift, my dear Alexandra. May you have
a long and fruitful union, though I could have wished
it were with me.'

'Ali, you fool.' He had always been a frightful tease,
and she opened the box. Inside was a jewel-encrusted
tiny dagger. 'It's beautiful, Ali. Thank you.' She beamed
up at him. But Jake was not so happy; she felt his fingers
dig into her waist.

'My wife does not take jewellery from any man except
me.' His icy blue eyes clashed with the brown of Ali's.

'So it should be,' Ali responded coolly. 'But if you
observe, it is a letter-knife to remind you both to keep
in touch.'

Ali left moments later, sweeping out of the hotel with
his bodyguard chasing after him. He had explained he
was sailing within the hour for home.

Jake turned Lexi into his arms and, relieving her of
the jewel box, slipped it in his pocket. 'That man wanted

you,' he said flatly, his intent gaze searching her upturned face. 'He is one of the wealthiest men in the
world, and you could have married him.'

'Don't be ridiculous,' she giggled. 'Ali is sought after
by the most gorgeous women in the world and delights
in letting them catch him, while his father despairs of
him ever settling down. He is just a boy and he likes to
tease.' And, suddenly feeling bold, she added, 'Haven't
you realised yet, Jake? There has only ever been you.'

'What!' He stared into her laughing eyes, and what
he saw there must have convinced him. 'God! Lexi, you
choose the damnedest place to make a confession like
that. We really need to talk.' He hugged her tight.

But at that moment they were accosted by Signor
Monicelli, and for the next few hours Lexi was floating
on Cloud Nine. She danced with the chef, Franco and
host of others but always after each dance Jake was there
to claim her.

Finding herself alone for a moment Lexi glanced
around the room. Poor Jake had been dragged by Anna
on to the dance-floor and she was trying to teach him
to cha-cha amid much laughter. Lexi smiled to herself
and carefully eased her way through the crowd and into
the foyer; she felt slightly dizzy, the heat and the noise
finally getting to her.

'Enjoying the party?' Lorraine appeared from behind
the Reception desk. 'I'm supposed to join in when Anna
remembers to come and relieve me, but frankly a rave-
up with all the staff isn't really good for business.'

Groaning inwardly, Lexi faced up to the other woman.
'It was Jake's idea,' she said swiftly. Whatever Lorraine
had meant to Jake in the past, Lexi was hoping against
hope it was over. Jake's insistence that they talk and the
way he had behaved today all pointed to that fact, and
she would not let Lorraine dampen her spirit.

'Yes, I know; he asked me to arrange it all. But personally I think it's a waste of money. I told him he was

a fool, but then all men are. Why should I worry? He pays me exceptionally well to do what he wants,' she taunted with a smile that did not reach her hard eyes.

'He is a very generous man,' Lexi said firmly. She did not like the assessing look in Lorraine's gaze as she moved to stand directly in front of her.

'What is it about you, Lexi?' Lorraine questioned almost to herself. 'You're beautiful. You and I could have been friends if you weren't a threat to my position in the company.' She put her long-nailed hand on Lexi's bare shoulder, her fingers biting into the flesh. 'You're intelligent, but you have one failing—you're the type of woman who needs a man. What a waste. Jake knows you are a gold-digger, and he'll drop you in the end, and I'll still be around, his right-hand man.'

Lexi stepped back. Lorraine as a friend! The woman must be mad. 'That's enough. I will not discuss my husband with you.' She refused to let the woman get to her. Tonight was Lexi's and Jake was hers, and, spinning on her heel, she flung over her shoulder, 'I'll send Anna out.' It was odd; Lexi realised that even before she knew about Jake and Lorraine, the woman had always made her uncomfortable, and she didn't think it was just jealousy. With a toss of her red hair she headed for the party but before she had gone three steps Jake was at her side.

'What was Lorraine saying?' Jake demanded curtly. 'Did she upset you?'

Sliding an arm around his neck and another around his waist, she pressed herself against him. 'No more than usual, in fact she wanted to be friends, would you believe?' she teased; she wanted nothing to spoil this night, and she wasn't going to let Lorraine's catty remarks hurt her.

'She touched you.' His dark eyes fell to the red mark on her naked shoulder. 'Did she hurt you?' The harsh demand in Jake's tone made Lexi lift her eyes to his.

'No, of course not. She didn't punch me out for being with you.' Lexi grinned, but Jake did not respond; instead his eyes narrowed with some undisclosed emotion.

'Look, I'm sorry if I upset your girlfriend——' She was not going to let anything spoil her party.

'She is not my girlfriend.' Jake cut her off, his handsome face harsh in the artificial light. 'She works for me, nothing more, though not for much longer, I think.' And, sliding an arm around Lexi's waist, he led her towards the dance-floor. 'I'm beginning to wonder...'

'Wonder what?' Lexi asked, secretly delighted at the suggestion that Jake and Lorraine might part company.

Jake, in a quick about-face, spun her around; his eyes, gleaming with devilish amusement, gazed down into hers as he swept her into his arms, and said, 'Wonder if I should serenade you.' And he burst into song.

She knew he had deliberately changed the subject, but she didn't care, and, entering into the mood, she began to giggle as he whirled her around and around. 'You're a terrible singer.'

'I know, but I do do something well...' he drawled sexily, one hand sliding down to her buttocks, he held her firmly against him. The band started to play a Latin love song, and slowly they circled the floor, touching from shoulder to knee, their bodies moving lazily as one. Jake nuzzled her ear and she melted in his arms.

CHAPTER TEN

AT LAST the crowd was thinning. Lexi breathed a sigh of contentment. It had been a lovely party, and, wriggling out of Jake's arms, she whispered, 'I need the powder-room.' But as she crossed the foyer Anna called out,

'Lexi, do you want to collect your tapes now?'

'Yes, sure.' Lexi had left her favourite tapes in Anna's room when she had been sharing it with her for a week. Quickly, she followed Anna around Reception and down the corridor to her room at the rear of the hotel.

Ten minutes later with the box of tapes tucked under her arm, Lexi slowly walked back to the foyer. She was sad at leaving her friends; she had had some good times at the Piccolo Paradiso she mused, but she nursed a secret feeling of hope that the best was yet to come. Jake wanted to talk, and she knew in her heart that this time it would be all right. She wasn't sure she was pregnant, but had taken care to drink only two glasses of champagne all evening. In any case, she hadn't needed the stimulus. An attractive, caring Jake was stimulus enough for her.

She stopped, her eyes widening in shocked disbelief; her hand went to her heart, pressing at her breast in a futile attempt to stop it breaking. At the end of the corridor, silhouetted by the stronger light of Reception, stood a couple wrapped in each others' arms; the man had his back to her but there was no mistaking it was Jake, and Lorraine. As she watched, his dark head bent. Lexi turned and ran back along the hall, her eyes blinded by tears.

She leaned against the wall and gulped in the warm night air, her heart pounding; the box of tapes fell unnoticed to the ground as she rubbed her knuckles in her eyes, trying to stem the tears. Taking a shaky breath she straightened, and gazed dazedly at her surroundings. She was in the staff car park at the back of the hotel.

She was shivering and yet it was a hot summer night. She looked up at the sky; a million stars glittered and sparkled in the midnight blue of the moonlit vastness. But the beauty of the scene was lost on her. It had happened again. Once more she had allowed herself to trust, to love, had wished for the moon! And for a while she had thought it was within her grasp. What a fool! Her hopes and dreams were shattered like a burst balloon.

Lexi had no notion how long she stood there; an icy chill pervaded the very marrow of her bones until finally she moved, stiffly like a robot, one foot in front of the other, but with no idea where she was going; she only knew she had to get away. Then she noticed it. Her little car was parked next to the car park exit. It looked abandoned, much the way she felt herself, she thought sadly. Automatically she tried the door and it opened; she slid into the driver's seat, her hand finding the ignition. The key had been left in place...

She turned on the engine, her foot pressing on the clutch and slipped it into first gear. But suddenly the door was wrenched open, a long hand reached over and cut off the ignition, another arm pressed across her chest as a strong hand hauled on the handbrake.

'No, you don't.' Lexi turned her tear-stained face at the harsh command, and saw Jake's towering form blocking the door. His eyes flashed with rage and a muscle jerked in his cheek. 'Get out of that car,' he snarled.

'Leave me alone,' she said, her voice breaking on a sob as she tried to prise his arm off her breast.

'Running to your Arab friend, were you?' Jake's face was murderous. 'You bitch.' His lips drew back from his teeth in a snarl of animal fury.

How like him to blame her! Lexi thought and, in a mercurial change of mood, anger overtaking her former despair, she beat at his arm, trying to break free. 'Let me go, don't touch me, I hate you...' she cried, all her hurt and anger bubbling to the surface; she thrashed around in the seat trying to dislodge his aggressive hold. 'You great brute. Let me go...' she screamed almost hysterically.

'Never,' he ground out through clenched teeth.

With a frightened animal's instinct for escape Lexi changed tactics and scrambled the other way. But with the speed of light Jake was in the car and flinging her back against the passenger seat.

His face was inches from her own, his eyes leaping with rage, his breathing harsh. 'You go anywhere near that Arab again,' he rasped menacingly, his strong hand sliding up her neck to encircle her throat, 'I'll kill you.' His rugged face was tight with demoniac anger, the muscle in his cheek jerking as he tried to control his fury and in that moment Lexi believed him.

'I wasn't running to Ali, I was running away from you,' she cried scathingly.

Jake stared down at her, his hand gradually relaxing its grip on her throat. 'So what's new?' he grated. She watched his massive chest heave as he took slow, deep gulps of air, fighting to regain his control until finally he moved back into the driving seat and, with one withering glance at Lexi's huddled form, he started the car.

She bit her lip. 'What do you think you're doing? This is my car. Your limousine will be waiting for you out front,' she snapped sarcastically.

'And take the chance of you disappearing again? No way, Lexi.'

She cast a venomous glance at his harsh profile; his face was taut, his hands gripping the steering-wheel as if his life depended on it. She opened her mouth to speak but the car squealed on two wheels out of the car park and Lexi was flung against Jake.

She straightened back in her seat, she had felt the rigid tension in his arm in his whole body as they had touched, and the same tension filled the intimate confines of the tiny car. She turned her head and looked out of the side window and realised they were bombing along Amalfi Drive at a speed she was sure the car had never been built to achieve. Her heart in her mouth, she stayed silent, frozen with fear.

He was taking her back to the villa, that much was obvious. Jake could make her stay, he could make her love him. She already did, and that would never change, she accepted the fact sadly; and up until tonight she had thought maybe they could make their marriage work. But now she knew categorically that she had been fooling herself; it was an impossibility.

Jake had broken her heart not once but twice. She might just be able to stick the pieces back and continue to function; she could try. But, if she stayed, his infidelities, especially with Lorraine, would chip away at her self-respect, her pride, and little by little chisel away at her bruised heart until there was nothing left but dust, nothing to mend. She couldn't allow it to happen. She wouldn't.

She glanced at Jake. His profile looked as though it was carved out of stone; she despised the sudden lurch in her pulse while recognising that he was a formidable man in every way. But surely even Jake could not watch her all the time. She would get her chance and run as far and as fast as she could. She had done it once and she could again. She had no other alternative...

The huge gates of the villa swung open in front of them and Lexi gave a sigh of relief; she could breathe again, the harrowing drive was over. But her relief was short-lived, as the car ground to a jarring halt at the front door, and Jake was around the car, the passenger door open, and his hand curving around her bare arm like a vice as he dragged her out.

'I can manage,' she said, jerking her arm free, and blindly she turned and dashed for the house and the safety of her room, but she had barely taken two steps into the hall before Jake caught her.

'What the hell are you trying to do to me, Lexi?' he grated, and with a savage movement swung her around to face him.

Lexi stared up at him. 'Me, Jake?' she screeched. She couldn't believe his outrageous accusation—to her mind it was the other way around—but she was astounded to note the stain of red running along his high cheekbones, the taut fury in his handsome face.

'Yes, you. Who the hell else is there?'

Lorraine for one! she almost cried, but Jake, without waiting for an answer, swept her up in his arms, and carried her straight into the salon. She lashed out at him, her hands connecting with his head and his broad back. 'Put me down,' she yelled furiously and he did, dropping her unceremoniously down on the velvet-covered sofa.

He towered over her, huge and menacing; she had never seen him so consumed with rage. His glittering eyes raked over her with a ruthless savagery that made her feel as if he could see through to her bones. She fumbled with the skirt of her dress that had ridden high over her thighs, exposing her shapely legs, and tried to get up.

'Don't bother.' Jake lowered his body on to the sofa beside her and her attempt to sit up was blocked by his hand roughly pushing her back. His eyes flared like blue flame with rage. 'I'll have it off you in a minute.' His hard body pinned her beneath him. 'If this is the only way I can have you, so be it...' he snarled, as his dark head bent and his mouth covered hers in a ravaging travesty of a kiss. His hand wrenched the bodice of her dress to her waist while his other hand entangled brutally in the back of her hair, insensitive to the hurt he was inflicting.

Lexi twisted and turned, her slender body bucking against him, trying to break free from his crazed assault on her susceptible senses. She reeled from the force of his kiss, then gasped as his mouth found the rosy peak of her breast. She rained blows down on his broad back, but, to her horror, long shudders rippled through her body as she felt herself succumbing to his persuasive mouth and hands.

'No, no.' And with one last frantic effort she grasped his head between her hands and tried to push him way. 'I will not let you do this to me. I won't, I swear I won't,' she repeated over and over again, like a sacred mantra. Tossing her head from side to side, her eyes closed tight, she screamed, 'No! No...'

'Stop it, stop it, Lexi.' Jake's voice penetrated her distraught mind and she realised she was virtually free. Jake was sitting on the side of the sofa, his face as black as thunder, but his blue eyes were strangely blank. 'You can relax. I'm not about to assault you, though you are the most maddening, complex female it has ever been my misfortune to meet. I want some answers, and I want them now...' The cold implacability in his tone was in direct contrast to the fierce tension she could sense in his hard body hovering over her. He had rested one arm on the back of the sofa, while with his other hand he deftly pulled her up to a sitting position and adjusted the bodice of her dress up over her breasts. 'With no distractions,' he murmured almost under his breath.

Lexi drew a deep, shuddering breath, her eyes clashing with Jake's, and she knew the moment of truth had come. She had been on the very edge of hysteria, and there was nothing left in her emotional bank.

'I thought you and I had reached some kind of understanding, a level of commitment since Pompeii, and tonight I was sure. Was I mistaken?' Jake demanded tautly.

'No,' she murmured with a weary shake of her head.

'So why the devil did you run away again?' He sounded infuriated and almost unaware of what he was saying. 'My first thought was, mercenary little bitch, she's decided that flaming Arab was a better bet. But in the car coming home, when I had time to calm down, I realised I was wrong. Wasn't I?'

'Yes,' Lexi confirmed quietly.

'For five years I considered you a gold-digger of the worst kind. I told myself I was well rid of you, but it didn't stop me wanting you. Then, when I heard the hotel where you worked was on the market, I saw a perfect opportunity to get you back but on my terms, and I took it. I'd have you as my wife again in my bed and under my control,' he declared his eyes searching her face grimly. 'I told myself, to hell with your mercenary tendencies, I was wealthy enough to indulge them.'

'Gee, thanks. A girl could get a swelled head listening to you.' The sarcasm hid the hurt his words caused her.

His gaze narrowed speculatively on her stiff, resentful features. 'Hold your sarcasm, Lexi, I haven't finished,' he commanded bluntly. 'The past two weeks I have been forced to accept that I was wrong. I discovered you've never touched your account in London, and you actually worked to live, not just as an excuse to meet wealthy men, and yet you said you left me for money. I have seen with my own eyes Ali, one of the world's wealthiest bachelors, drool over you, but you were planning to marry Dante, a man I could buy and sell a million times over.' His hand closed over hers, his thumb rubbing the glittering ring on her finger. 'I don't like a mystery; I want some answers and fast.'

'Maybe I didn't leave you because I wanted money,' was as far as she was prepared to go in enlightening him. To reveal her real reason after seeing him with Lorraine again was not something she dared contemplate. She had her pride if nothing else...

'I know that years ago I let you down, Lexi, and broke my promise to you, but I thought you cared enough for me, were mature enough to understand.' Jake thrust a hand through his tumbled hair. 'I never expected you to take off then or now... Talk to me, Lexi, make me understand.'

Lexi stared at him. He had said as much before, and she had been unable to comprehend his reasoning. Perhaps because secretly, deep in her subconscious, she had not wanted to believe she could love a man so totally bereft of any morality. Looking away from his too penetrating eyes she said, in a voice devoid of all emotion, 'I understand I shouldn't have run away.' She tried to stand but Jake, with a brief tug on her hand, forced her back down beside him.

'You're not going anywhere until we have talked this through.' His dark eyes held hers, an intensely speculative look in their indigo depths. 'So, why did you run away, not once but twice?' he prompted.

'If I had stayed in England I could have been divorced and free within weeks. It's my one big regret in life, apart from meeting you in the first place,' she said curtly, an icy calm possessing her. She stared up into his harsh face. He still had her hand in his, but his other arm was curved over the back of the sofa, not touching her but effectively encircling her.

'I very much doubt that,' he drawled cynically. 'But do carry on, this is beginning to get interesting.'

Interesting. He had ruined her life, and had the audacity... Suddenly all her hurt, all her anger came streaming out.

'I was a naïve fool when I married you. I knew you wanted Forest Manor, but my mistake was in thinking you wanted me more. I discovered the truth that night at the London apartment. It was ironic really; for weeks I had suffered from hormonal depression after the miscarriage but that morning Dr Bell had convinced me to snap out of it.' She looked at Jake, not really seeing him. 'I caught the train to London, happy for the first time in ages, my passport in my purse, and dreaming of a wedding anniversary in Paris.'

Jake's only reaction was to tighten his grip on her hand.

'Instead, I found you and your mistress, virtually naked, calmly discussing how you could tell your poor little wife you had broken your marriage vow, and wanted your freedom, and would I settle for cash...?'

Jake's head snapped back. 'You what?' The words were rasped out hoarsely, but Lexi ignored his aghast query.

'Of course I said I'd take the money. I had some pride left, though not enough to drink champagne to your future happiness. But you know the real irony, Jake?' she asked with a harsh laugh. 'I would have sold you the house for the price of my father's debts without a qualm. Contrary to your opinion of my mercenary characteristics, I have never had any great desire for material things. So you see, our marriage was totally unnecessary.'

There was a silence, and she could hear the ticking of the ornate ormolu clock on the mantelpiece. She glanced at it. Almost two, her mind registered, as her gaze swung back to Jake. The expression on his ruggedly handsome face would have been laughable if the moment had not been so tense. His face was grey beneath its tan, his wide mouth parted in an incredulous gasp; he looked absolutely stupefied.

Well, why shouldn't he hear some home-truths? Lexi thought with bitter resentment. He had been the one calling the tune for far too long. 'As for your latest attempt at a reconciliation, Luigi was right. Nothing changes. I saw you and Lorraine tonight in each other's arms, and realised, much as I value my friendship with Signor Monicelli, I am not prepared to give my life for it.'

Jake dropped her hand and grabbed her by the shoulders, pushing her against the back of the sofa. He stared down into her pale face as though he had never seen her before, and when he spoke it was as if each word was forced out of him. 'Am I to understand that you left me because you thought I only wanted your house, and I was having an affair with Lorraine? Have I got that right?'

'Not thought, knew,' Lexi said scathingly.

'Oh, my God. I knew we needed to talk but I never realised...what you imagined... What a low opinion you must have of me...' His rich voice deepened with a strange urgency. 'Lexi, you've got it all wrong.'

'I don't think so.' She tried to sit up but Jake wouldn't allow it. Instead he swung her up and across his thigh to hold her on his lap like a small child, a strong arm firmly around her waist.

'Let me go.' Held in his arms close to his hard warmth, his strong thighs beneath her, she was far too susceptible to him, and she tried to slide off his lap, but Jake was having none of it. 'Sit still and for once in your life listen,' he demanded hardily, but, with an oddly gentle gesture, he brushed the tangle of her red hair from the side of her face before curving his hand around her leg.

Lexi stopped struggling. She would hear what he had to say. She didn't have much choice, she was trapped, but she didn't have to believe him...

'Do you remember that night when you arrived at the apartment?'

'Yes,' she said curtly. She would never forget.

'I asked you if you had heard all our conversation and you agreed.'

'I heard enough.' Lexi glared up at him. His betrayal was an ache in her heart. 'And I saw: the woman was wearing my robe.'

'For the very simple reason, if you cast your mind back, that there was a hell of a storm that night and we were both soaked to the skin. There is no way on this earth I could ever have an affair with Lorraine; her preference is for other women, and always has been.'

'What?' Lexi gasped. Her violet eyes clashed with his. He wasn't joking, he was deadly serious. 'You expect me to believe that Lorraine...' As excuses went it was a classic, but could she believe it? He was right about the rain. A brief memory of when they were on honeymoon prompted her to ask, 'In Paris, when I asked if you and she had had an affair—was that why you laughed? And I never got the joke.'

'Exactly. I should have told you, but I thought Lorraine's sexual preference was her own affair.'

'But I heard you tell Lorraine you were breaking your wedding vows.' However Jake tried to colour his story, that fact was unmistakable.

'No, Lexi, you heard me say I was breaking my promise to you. But what you obviously didn't hear was the first part of the conversation.' His sober gaze held hers captive as he continued. 'It had nothing to do with our marriage, but none the less it doesn't reflect very well on me.'

Lexi tensed, fearing what was to follow.

'I promised you that, when Forest Manor was converted to a hotel, you would always have a home there. But unfortunately it wasn't possible.'

Inexplicably, a tiny glimmer of something very like hope ignited in Lexi's heart. She squirmed on his lap and, lifting one hand, placed it on his chest urging him to continue. 'And? Carry on.'

'Sit still and I will,' Jake commented with a very masculine groan. 'Yes, well, the bottom had dropped out of the property market and I had sunk all my cash into the Docklands venture. The only good news was the meeting with Mr Stewart, the American I was dining with the night we lost our baby.' He hugged her tighter for a moment. 'It hurt me more than you knew, Lexi.'

'I think I do know, after Pompeii,' she confessed.

'Anyway, that night Mr Stewart loved the hotel, but—and this is the hard part—he didn't want to lease the rooms, but made me an offer to buy the hotel outright. I resisted at first. I didn't dare discuss it with you, not when you were ill and so depressed. The night you burst in on Lorraine and me we were arguing over the sale of Forest Manor. I knew it made sound business sense to liquidate some of my assets, and the hotel was the simplest one to dispose of; the offer was lying on my desk. I couldn't refuse. But it meant breaking my promise to you. I felt a heel, but there was no other way out. It would save the construction firm and solve my cash-flow problem.'

Lexi's violet eyes widened in horror as the full extent of her mistake dawned on her. 'You...I...' She could not find the words to express her feelings. She believed Jake. It all made perfect sense. While she had convinced herself Jake had broken his sacred wedding vow and wanted a divorce, he had simply been afraid to tell her that his business was in trouble and Forest Manor had to be sold. Maybe if she had not been so depressed about the miscarriage she would have recognised the signs—looking back he had given plenty of hints that business was difficult—but in her pregnant state he had not wanted to worry her, and afterwards she had been so wrapped in her grief that she had not listened to him at all.

'When I thought you were discussing breaking your marriage vow,' Lexi reasoned slowly, 'you were actually talking about the promise you made to keep the house!' she exclaimed, the enormity of her mistake too much to take in. 'Five years... at cross purposes...' The hurt! If only she had waited, allowed him to explain... With a flash of insight she realised something else. 'My father's debt. How much did it finally come to?' She had never asked at the time, but she had heard the rumours since of Lloyds names going bankrupt trying to pay off the appalling losses after a string of disasters.

'You don't need to know,' Jake said firmly.

'Please.' Her hand moved agitatedly against his chest. 'If we are to make anything of our marriage we have to have truth between us.' A flush stained her cheeks as she realised what she had proposed.

His hand covered hers where it lay on his shirt, his long fingers lacing with hers. 'The truth.' His eyes flared darkly. 'I'd do anything in the world for our marriage, Lexi,' he said emphatically, and pressed a swift hard kiss on her parted lips. She felt herself relax against him, then immediately went rigid in his arms when he mentioned a sum that made her head spin.

'Oh, my God! That much.'

'Yes, but not to worry, I can easily afford it now, but at the time it was touch and go for a while. That's why, when you told me that night you had heard everything and agreed, I was so relieved and delighted you didn't mind losing the manor, I suggested the celebratory drink. I couldn't believe it when you said you would take your share of the money and never wanted to see me again. For a few seconds I believed you were the gold-digger Lorraine had tried to warn me about before we married, and I yelled at you. But it didn't last for long. I thought you would come back to me. I told myself, Be patient, she's still depressed, let her have a holiday. When it finally dawned on me that I had lost you for good, I decided Lorraine must have been right all along: you were only after money.'

She saw the pain in his dark eyes, and she lifted her hand to stroke his cheek. 'I never cared about money and not much about the house. It was only you I wanted, Jake; I loved you, you were my life. I would have lived in a tent if you'd asked me,' she blurted. Still reeling with the shock of his revelation, she didn't realise what she was confessing.

'Past tense, Lexi?' Jake queried softly, and, catching her chin between his finger and thumb, he tilted her face up to his. 'I love you, I always have; the last five years have been hell without you. Will you give me another chance to let me try and win your love? Please, Lexi.'

The flicker of hope in her heart burst into a glorious flame. Jake, her husband, vulnerable and pleading for her love, was like a dream come true, and she wanted to believe it. Curled on his lap, his strength and warmth enveloping her, she almost did, but still a niggling doubt persisted. 'Lorraine—she was in your arms tonight. I saw you, Jake; are you sure she...'

Jake's strong arm hugged her to his broad chest as he said urgently, 'Tonight, in Reception, seeing you and Lorraine together, her hand on you.' His dark brows drew together in a frown. 'She hurt you, and that I will not tolerate, and if I'm being brutally honest I saw something in her eyes when she looked at you that gave me the same gut-wrenching jealousy I got when I saw you and Dante together, and it made me wonder how I could have been so stupid.'

'You mean Lorraine fancies me?' And she laughed out loud at his outrageous suggestion.'

'I don't know, but I'm not taking the chance.'

'But you more or less admitted she was your mistress when you insisted we resume our marriage.' Yet Jake's explanation didn't shock her as much as it should have done. Lorraine had always made her flesh creep.

A rueful grin flashed across Jake's sensuous mouth. 'Self-defence! I'm not proud of myself, but, seeing you with Dante, I wasn't above letting you think I was having an affair. The truth is that you are the only woman I have made love to in five long years.'

Lexi stared into his dark eyes, her heart pounding like a drum, and what she saw in the glittering depths almost convinced her he was telling the truth. Jake celibate for five years was a stunning revelation. 'But I saw you kiss her, Jake . . .'

'No,' he denied. 'But let me tell you about Lorraine, so there can be no doubt left in your mind. Much as I value Lorraine's business ability, there is no way I can stand by and watch her hurt you.'

'Lorraine has never liked me, but she didn't hurt me,' Lexi said honestly.

'You're too soft-hearted.' Jake dropped a swift kiss on her forehead. 'And I let pity and stupid teenage guilt blind me to Lorraine's obsessive character.'

Lexi tensed at the word guilt. Had Jake been involved with Lorraine? She still did not quite credit his tale of Lorraine's sexuality. She was sure the woman fancied Jake whether he knew it or not. But then, she was prejudiced, she thought ruefully, sure the woman didn't live who couldn't fancy Jake.

'As sixteen-year-olds, Lorraine and I were in the same class at school. She wasn't a friend. In fact her only friend was a girl called Pat. They were both real lookers, but never went out with any boys, and, as teenage boys do, we teased them unmercifully about being gay, which I might add they freely admitted to. It was also common knowledge that Lorraine's father was a drunk who beat up both her and her mother. On more than one occasion she appeared in class with a black eye.'

'Oh, the poor girl.'

'Yes, well, years later, when Lorraine applied for a job with my company, I remembered her and my own

182 NOTHING CHANGES LOVE

insensitive teasing as a teenager. She told me her friend
Pat had been killed in a car crash some months earlier
and I felt sorry for her. Plus I had had an embarrassing
experience with my last secretary imagining she was in
love with me and leaving in tears. Lorraine's qualifi-
cations weren't great, but at least I could be sure she
wouldn't spend all day making cow's eyes at me, so I
gave her the job. She's worked hard for me ever since.
But tonight I realised something I should have recognised six years ago, when she first tried to convince me
you were only after a wealthy husband. She had become
far too ambitious, or perhaps possessive is a better word,
of her position in my company.'

Lexi allowed herself a wry smile at Jake's arrogant
confession about his secretary falling in love with him,
but listened intently as he went on.

'Later, when you lost our baby, I should have got rid
of her then. But with typical masculine arrogance I
thought I understood the poor woman. An abusive
father! It was only natural she was the way she was. I
know now I should have left the psychiatry to the
professionals, but at the time I thought, for someone
with her family background to forget the message from
the hospital was excusable. Family life was of no interest
to her. But tonight I wondered how I could have been
such a fool. Anyone, male or female, whatever their
sexual preference or family background, receiving such
a life-and-death message would never have forgotten. I
have to conclude she did it deliberately. I can't tell you
how sorry I am, Lexi. I was an idiot.'

Lexi had thought at the time that Lorraine had forgotten the message simply to hurt her, but she had been
too ill, too depressed to make an issue of it.

'What you saw earlier in the foyer, Lexi, was our
parting. I had just told Lorraine I was transferring her
to the New York branch, and she knew it was more a
demotion than a promotion. I suggested if she didn't

like it, she should consider looking for a job elsewhere, and she resigned. I realised that over the years her efficiency had blinded me to the fact she had become far too interfering in my private and personal life. Lorraine kissed me goodbye, but I swear it is the closest she has ever been to me in all the time I have known her, and it was just a kiss on the cheek.'

Lexi hadn't actually seen the kiss, and she wanted to believe Jake's version of events.

'You do believe me, Lexi?' Jake asked urgently.

'Yes. Yes, I believe you.' It was too incredible to be anything other than the truth, she thought dazedly, and reaching up she gently outlined Jake's wide, sensuous mouth with one finger, her eyes shining with relief and love...aching for his kiss.

But doggedly Jake caught her hand and held it firmly against his broad chest. 'Today in Naples I signed the contract to buy back Forest Manor. You can have your old home back, Lexi, anything you want. If you will stay with me, I can make you love me again, I know it, if you will give me the chance.'

Lexi, her eyes moist with tears, gazed into the wary blue depths of Jake's. 'That wasn't necessary, Jake. You don't have to make me. I do. Even when I thought I hated you...I loved you. You're more than enough for me.'

'Thank God.' His lips captured hers in a kiss like no other, soft and tender and promising everything. When he finally ended the kiss he grinned wickedly down into her flushed face. 'I might as well confess, I did have an ulterior motive. I thought, along with the Piccolo Paradiso, it has the makings of a successful hotel chain with you as the administrator. I figured if I couldn't win your love at least I would be assured of keeping your interest, keeping you by my side.'

Lexi chuckled in delight. Jake, whom she had thought the world's worse chauvinist, was offering her not only his love but a career as well. 'I love you, Jake Taylor, devious as you are.'

'Darling Lexi,' Jake muttered, his voice husky with passion. 'My wife. I love you and I'll never let you down again, I swear.' And for the next few moments he set about convincing her very thoroughly.

When Jake finally allowed her to draw breath again somehow she was lying on the sofa, with his large body covering hers, his elbows supporting his weight either side of her slender body and his dark gaze lingered, oddly serious, on the pale perfection of her face. 'You do believe me, Lexi? Trust me? I need that.'

She looked at him all her love plain to see in the deepening purple depths of her huge eyes. 'Yes, my love.' She cupped his hard jaw in the palm of her hand and added with a tinge of sadness, 'And I'm sorry. Jake, this has all been my fault; if I had trusted you more, if I had allowed you to explain, we would never have wasted five years.'

'So why are we wasting time?' Jake rasped, one long finger tracing the soft curve of her breasts. But this time Lexi called a halt.

Suddenly it seemed imperative he knew how she had felt at the time. 'I think because I had lost our child I felt guilty, a failure and not really entitled to be happy; I was confused, and finding you and Lorraine together was the last straw. For a long time after we parted I told myself I hated you, I even thought losing the baby was a sign that our marriage was not meant to be,' she confessed simply.

'No, Lexi. You must never think that, never blame yourself,' Jake said adamantly. 'If anyone was at fault it was me. After a couple of months I decided you were a gold-digger, and I was well rid of you. When Carl Bradshaw showed me your photograph it only confirmed my suspicion. Carl omitted to tell me you were working, and I thought you were a guest at an expensive hotel on the look-out for a wealthy partner. Even so, I couldn't resist ringing the hotel and asking for Mrs Taylor. When I was told there was no guest registered in that name I assumed you must have left the hotel shortly after Carl, probably still looking for a meal-ticket and so confirming, to my mind, your mercenary tendencies.'

Her hands fell from his face. 'A guest! But you said you knew where I was all the time.'

A wry smile curved his hard mouth. 'So I stretched the truth a bit—a weak attempt to show you I didn't care. In fact, I didn't dare question Carl about you, because I didn't want to remind him of you, in case he decided to try and win you himself. It was only ten months ago, when he was safely married that I had the nerve to ask him about you once more, and that was when I discovered my mistake and realised you had been working in the hotel... I immediately checked, this time asking under both Taylor and Laughton, and discovered you were still at the Piccolo Paradiso. I flew straight out to Naples and bought the villa—— '

'You bought it?' she cut in. 'But you said your father left it to you.'

'So I lied.' Jake had the grace to look ashamed but not for long. 'I didn't want to admit that as soon as I knew you were still in Italy I went straight out and bought a house to be near you.'

'Oh, Jake.' She could not believe this vulnerable man was the ruthless Jake of the past few weeks.

'I kept telling myself I didn't love you, and you weren't worth my regard. But all the time in the back of my mind was the desire to get you back. You have no idea how many times I drove past the hotel hoping to see you, but at the same time telling myself I hated you. And I was determined to make you pay for all the pain you had caused me.'

'Hence the blackmail,' Lexi murmured, lifting her arms to encircle his neck, and linking her hands together she urged his head down. 'You would not really have pulled out of the deal with Signor Monicelli.' She kissed him softly, swiftly.

'No,' he breathed against her mouth. 'After all, he kept you safe for me. But I was desperate; I found out you had a boyfriend, Dante, and it looked like getting serious, time was running out. The final blow was when I was in America on business and got the fax from my solicitor saying you were asking for a divorce. I knew I had to act or lose you forever.'

'That isn't possible; I love you too much.' Lexi rushed to reassure him.

'Now I'm beginning to believe it, darling.' He bent to kiss her again.

'Wait a minute.' Lexi pulled back. 'You speak Italian, so was your father Italian?' If he had lied about the house...

Jake started to grin. 'I haven't the slightest idea. I took a crash course in the language. I told myself if you love Italy so much then so must I, and if it pleases you to think of me as half-Italian, then that is what I am.'

Lexi couldn't get angry with him; instead a beaming smile illuminated her small face at the thought of the lengths he had gone to for her. 'As long as you're mine I don't care.'

'I am.' Jake gathered her close, a shuddering sigh shaking his powerful body, and she thought she heard him say 'always' before his mouth possessed hers with a poignant hunger that left no room for doubt.

'I refuse to make love to you on the sofa,' Jake murmured throatily. 'This calls for a celebration—champagne and the master bedroom, at the very least.'

Lexi tilted her head to one side, and pretended to consider. 'Will you sleep with me, though, I ask myself.' A tiny smile traced her full lips, but she held her breath as she waited for his answer.

Jake growled huskily, 'I didn't dare before, in case I blurted out my love for you, but now I intend to sleep, eat, drink with you. The way I feel right now, I will never let you out of my bed again.'

Her last doubt resolved. 'Promises, promises,' she teased as he swung her up in his arms and carried her upstairs. Gently placing her in the centre of the huge bed, he lay down beside her and kissed her willing lips. 'I love you, Jake,' she whispered against his mouth.

He leant up on one elbow and, cupping her chin in his hand, a film of moisture glazing his deep blue eyes, he murmured huskily, 'I don't deserve you, Lexi, you're beautiful inside and out,' he groaned. 'But I swear, nothing and nobody will ever come between us again; you can trust me with your life in this world and the next.'

'You are my world,' Lexi whispered and emotion flared in her violet eyes, turning them to deep purple as his mouth covered hers, kissing her with a deep, possessive passion that had her clinging to him.

Carefully he slipped her clothes from her body, scattering kisses over her melting flesh as he stripped off his own. Then they reached for each other, laughing, teasing, loving, at last free to celebrate openly with love in the sensual exploration of every single inch of each other, all the sweet, secret erogenous zones, until finally they joined as one in a rapturous acclamation of their love.

On Monday morning, Jake, with his arm firmly around Lexi's shoulder, stood glowering at the customs official behind his desk at Naples Airport.

'You realise, Lexi, that we're hopelessly late? That guide at Pompeii wasn't wrong with his "nothing changes". I'm not surprised the people were petrified in stone. It probably took them all afternoon to even decide the volcano had erupted if this chap is anything to go by. He's been reading the passports for at least ten minutes.'

'Oh, Jake, that's a terrible thing to say.' But she could not stop the chuckle that escaped her. 'Especially from a man who has just spent the last thirty-six hours in bed,' she teased with an impish smile at his frowning countenance.

'I did have some help.' His frown lifted as he gazed adoringly down at her. 'And it's true that nothing could ever change my love for you.'

The customs official handed back Jake's passport, and then, turning to Lexi, his black eyes gleaming appreciatively, gave her her own passport with a broad grin and, 'Have a good journey, *signorina*.'

Lexi repaid him with a brilliant smile, just before Jake grabbed her passport from her hand and hustled her through the departure gate.

'Some things have to change, and your damn passport is one of them. I'm not having total strangers assuming you're single, and openly ogling my wife...'

'Yes, Jake,' she meekly agreed, a secretive gleam in her lovely eyes; and why not? She had it all: the man she loved, the hope of a baby, and a great career to look forward to, if she wanted it...

PRIZE SURPRISE SWEEPSTAKES!

This month's prize:

BEAUTIFUL WEDGWOOD CHINA!

This month, as a special surprise, we're giving away a bone china dinner service for eight by Wedgwood**, one of England's most prestigious manufacturers!

Think how beautiful your table will look, set with lovely Wedgwood china in the casual Countryware pattern! Each five-piece place setting includes dinner plate, salad plate, soup bowl and cup and saucer.

The facing page contains two Entry Coupons (as does every book you received this shipment). Complete and return *all* the entry coupons; **the more times you enter, the better your chances of winning!**

Then keep your fingers crossed, because you'll find out by September 15, 1995 if you're the winner!

Remember: The more times you enter, the better your chances of winning!*

PWW KAL

PRIZE SURPRISE
SWEEPSTAKES

OFFICIAL ENTRY COUPON

This entry must be received by: AUGUST 30, 1995
This month's winner will be notified by: SEPTEMBER 15, 1995

YES, I want to win the Wedgwood china service for eight! Please enter me in the drawing and let me know if I've won!

Name_____

Address _____ Apt. _____

City   State/Prov.   Zip/Postal Code

Account #_____

Return entry with invoice in reply envelope.

© 1995 HARLEQUIN ENTERPRISES LTD.   CWW KAL

PRIZE SURPRISE
SWEEPSTAKES

OFFICIAL ENTRY COUPON

This entry must be received by: AUGUST 30, 1995
This month's winner will be notified by: SEPTEMBER 15, 1995

YES, I want to win the Wedgwood china service for eight! Please enter me in the drawing and let me know if I've won!

Name_____

Address _____ Apt. _____

City   State/Prov.   Zip/Postal Code

Account #_____

Return entry with invoice in reply envelope.

© 1995 HARLEQUIN ENTERPRISES LTD.   CWW KAL

OFFICIAL RULES

PRIZE SURPRISE SWEEPSTAKES 3448

NO PURCHASE OR OBLIGATION NECESSARY

Three Harlequin Reader Service 1995 shipments will contain respectively, coupons for entry into three different prize drawings, one for a Panasonic 31" wide-screen TV, another for a 5-piece Wedgwood china service for eight and the third for a Sharp ViewCam camcorder. To enter any drawing using an Entry Coupon, simply complete and mail according to directions.

There is no obligation to continue using the Reader Service to enter and be eligible for any prize drawing. You may also enter any drawing by hand printing the words "Prize Surprise," your name and address on a 3"x5" card and the name of the prize you wish that entry to be considered for (i.e., Panasonic wide-screen TV, Wedgwood china or Sharp ViewCam). Send your 3"x5" entries via first-class mail (limit: one per envelope) to: Prize Surprise Sweepstakes 3448, c/o the prize you wish that entry to be considered for, P.O. Box 1315, Buffalo, NY 14269-1315, USA or P.O. Box 610, Fort Erie, Ontario L2A 5X3, Canada.

To be eligible for the Panasonic wide-screen TV, entries must be received by 6/30/95; for the Wedgwood china, 8/30/95; and for the Sharp ViewCam, 10/30/95.

Winners will be determined in random drawings conducted under the supervision of D.L. Blair, Inc., an independent judging organization whose decisions are final, from among all eligible entries received for that drawing. Approximate prize values are as follows: Panasonic wide-screen TV ($1,800); Wedgwood china ($840) and Sharp ViewCam ($2,000). Sweepstakes open to residents of the U.S. (except Puerto Rico) and Canada, 18 years of age or older. Employees and immediate family members of Harlequin Enterprises, Ltd., D.L. Blair, Inc., their affiliates, subsidiaries and all other agencies, entities and persons connected with the use, marketing or conduct of this sweepstakes are not eligible. Odds of winning a prize are dependent upon the number of eligible entries received for that drawing. Prize drawing and winner notification for each drawing will occur no later than 15 days after deadline for entry eligibility for that drawing. Limit: one prize to an individual, family or organization. All applicable laws and regulations apply. Sweepstakes offer void wherever prohibited by law. Any litigation within the province of Quebec respecting the conduct and awarding of the prizes in this sweepstakes must be submitted to the Regies des loteries et Courses du Quebec. In order to win a prize, residents of Canada will be required to correctly answer a time-limited arithmetical skill-testing question. Value of prizes are in U.S. currency.

Winners will be obligated to sign and return an Affidavit of Eligibility within 30 days of notification. In the event of noncompliance within this time period, prize may not be awarded. If any prize or prize notification is returned as undeliverable, that prize will not be awarded. By acceptance of a prize, winner consents to use of his/her name, photograph or other likeness for purposes of advertising, trade and promotion on behalf of Harlequin Enterprises, Ltd., without further compensation, unless prohibited by law.

For the names of prizewinners (available after 12/31/95), send a self-addressed, stamped envelope to: Prize Surprise Sweepstakes 3448 Winners, P.O. Box 4200, Blair, NE 68009.

RPZ KAL